GETTING IT WRONG

LONDON

JUSTIN SWINGLE

adapted from the screenplay

LEWARO ROAD

1

THE MIRROR HANGING next to his door was exactly where it was when Peter took the room at Mrs. Chapman's, not far from Victoria station. Peter never moved it. He didn't like change; it was merely a distraction from what was truly important to him—writing his novel.

Each morning, Peter paused to glance at himself in the mirror and check his shirt buttons to make sure they were buttoned all the way up to his throat. He wore his drab gray shirt every day at the library where he worked. Well, he wore it everyday, period. Always buttoned up tight.

He stood at the door of his room for a moment looking at his watch before going down for breakfast. He never liked being early or late—just on time. Downstairs, Mrs. Chapman always had his tea and toast ready precisely at seven o'clock. She knew that was the way Peter liked it. Not early, never late, just there for him.

"Peter, you never have any of this nice marmalade on your toast."

Mrs. Chapman pushed the pot of marmalade towards him along with a motherly smile.

He replied with a smile and pushed it back again.

"No, Mrs. Chapman. Plain is fine."

"Have you ever been late? I mean to the library?" she asked.

Peter was perplexed. *Have I ever been late anywhere?* he pondered. It hardly seemed likely.

"No, Mrs. Chapman. Always on time. Never late, never early."

Again, he checked the top button of his shirt. It was secure. The morning was progressing as it should.

"But what if it rains?" she asked.

"I never thought about that." He replied. "It rains most days this month, doesn't it?"

At that, Peter grabbed his toast and rushed for the door in case it was raining. He didn't like being late.

It was February, and London's streets were still considerably dark that early. Peter moved through the deep shadows headed for Victoria station, where the tube would take him to the central library. He'd worked there since the end of the war. At the library, the doors always opened at nine and closed at precisely six. There no one cared about his drab gray shirt as the dim lights made everything look a bit gray. But then again, he'd never notice had they.

It was London's oldest and largest library. It was so old, in fact, that the floors creaked when he pushed his cart down the long aisles. This is certainly the place where one could get lost but probably not realize it until closing time. At least Peter wondered if such was possible.

Each morning Peter stacked his cart from the wooden box where returned books were left to be shelved. Shelving books wasn't as boring as one might think as each aisle was filled with new adventures with travel at one end and Victorian novels around the corner stack. He knew where everything was because he'd worked there so long, or at least it seemed like a long time to Peter. In these long rows of racks Peter could get lost in his thoughts, never worrying about being early or late because real time did not exist in his daydreams. There, everything so easily floated on the power of his imagination.

On a typical day, and after glancing up and down the aisles for his boss, Head Librarian Woods, he'd pick up a book that he'd been secretly treating himself to a page or two read a day. He loved *Outlander* by Diana Gabaldon. There was once a time when it had been checked out, which annoyed Peter. Still, he was halfway through the novel, but that day, he'd barely read the first paragraph of a new chapter when

Mrs. Woods walked up. He quickly shelved his read and made himself appear busy. But even in the shadowy aisles she knew what people were really up to. *Didn't she?* Peter wondered.

"Peter, isn't that the same cart of books you were pushing earlier?"

"No, Mrs. Woods. Books tend to look alike in this light."

She bent to glance closer at his cart.

"I see the titles also appear alike, but probably only in this light, I'm sure."

Mrs. Woods rolled her eyes and walked on. Peter took a deep breath, and when Mrs. Woods had progressed down the aisle far enough, he reached down to the lowest shelf on his cart and pulled his notebook from hiding. Opening it to the first page, he felt a sense of pride when he looked at the title page. It read "Novel by Peter Tinsley." Well, it yet had no title. That would come later. Then, with no one looking over his shoulder, Peter scribbled a few lines after pausing to contemplate how the warrior Jamie Fraser in *Outlander*, might teach Claire love like she'd never known? Well, Peter thought, when he figured it out, he'd put it in his own novel. But then again, who knows how love works? Perhaps it's one of those questions that's always chasing after an answer that's just out of reach. But what if love doesn't really work—it only happens? Perhaps a bit like miracles. Well, Peter was about to find out.

* * *

Things all started on one of those rainy days London is so known for. The library always got crowded early on wet days as even months after the war, there weren't many jobs. Where else could one wile away the hours for free?

Maggie didn't have a job. Every day, she would make her way to the library, where she pulled out every book that might have pictures of film stars, particularly American movie stars as their photos made them appear as though their polished faces glowed in the celluloid dark with eyelashes so long, they made shadows over their faces—both men and women. *How can I become one of these goddesses?* Maggie wondered? She pulled out her compact and applied a coat of red lipstick. That surely had to be a step in the right direction. The close-up of

Joan Crawford's glossy lips suggested she was on the path to stardom. But how many twists and turns to reach the stars? That was yet to come.

Late that morning, Peter slid his notebook back on the bottom of his cart and went back to shelving his books. As he pushed his cart up and down the long aisles, he was still pondering how the mighty Scotsman Jamie, could teach Claire how to love when he noticed this woman sitting in the other side of study hall. In front of her was the largest stack of books of anyone using the hall that day. He rolled his cart to the racks behind where she sat and pulled a book out so he could get a better glimpse of this creature with lips like a movie star. Suddenly Maggie noticed Peter and slung a wink his way. He ran for cover. Surely, Claire didn't just wink at Jamie, and that made his knees weak. Warriors don't have weak knees, do they? But then again, if Claire didn't wink at Jamie, then what device did she utilize to capture his attention? Peter slid the book back, and rolled off to shelf his cart of books. Strangely, the woman's smile seemed to haunt him as though she was somehow following him through the racks. Is that even possible? Peter looked behind to see.

After rolling up and down the aisles, and with what seemed like a hundred books returned to their proper places, it was nearing six o'clock and the library would soon be closing. Mrs. Woods had given Peter the task of informing patrons when it was near to closing time. He took his assignment seriously; after all, he would be representing the largest library in London. Peter drifted back to the study hall and eventually made his way to the woman with the stack of books.

"It's near six o'clock." Peter whispered to the creature with the red lips. But she never looked up from her book. He stood in the silence waiting. *Why didn't she respond?* he wondered? *Did she not hear him?* Finally, she paused from flipping pages and looked up.

"It sure enough is," she said. "But only for a minute or two… or three. How long can it be near six o'clock? Did they ever figure that out? Go find out."

With that this woman flipped to another page along with her attention.

What? How could Peter not wonder if she was from the continent? Over there people didn't understand the way things were meant to be, as well as the English. After all, hadn't she phrased the question as if it couldn't possibly have an answer? Peter even wondered what she'd truly said? Made no sense. *Is she French, then? Must be.* She simply didn't understand English, he reasoned.

Maggie turned another page and then paused to clarify for this obviously perplexed looking young man in the drab shirt.

"And you know, anyone can hold their breath that long. Watch!"

Maggie took a gulp of air, plugged her nose, and held it until she turned red.

Peter wondered what Mrs. Woods would think of this demonstration? What if she thought he'd strangled a patron until her lips turned cherry red?

Still, Maggie had better things to do, and went back to breathing naturally and the book on movie stars. Jean Harlow stared up at her, glad she'd returned. It can be lonely being a movie star. They resumed their thoughts together which carried them aimlessly to where time was never a concern as clocks simply did not exist in the celluloid heavens.

"The library is closing," Peter announced once again.

"Oh, is that what all your six o'clock fuss was about?"

"What?" was all Peter could get out.

He wondered if this patron plugged her nose again if she'd pass out and drop to the floor? How could this be happening to him at closing time? His palms got sweaty at the thought. Then the woman who looked like a movie star winked again.

"Yeah? Thought you were some kind of perv peeking through the books at me. I saw you, you know."

Perv, did she say? There's only pervs in Italy, he thought, *and likely France. Certainly not in England.*

"The library is closing," he repeated a tiny bit louder; after all, he was the official announcer that the library was closing for the day.

"Sit down here."

She gestured to the seat next to her.

"I want to show you all these move stars. You can help me decide if the boys are prettier than the girls. We'll start on page one. Sit."

Of course, Peter didn't sit down. All the same, the woman went on flipping the glossy pages ever so slowly as though the library was unlikely to ever close.

Peter had never faced such a conundrum. He felt the top button of his shirt to ascertain if it was properly buttoned and took a deep breath as he waited to see what might happen. Well, nothing did. *Wasn't his voice official-sounding*, he wondered?

"The library is closing…"

Peter wondered what Mrs. Woods would say about a patron defying closing at the proper time? Of course, it had never happened. Certainly not any time after the Norman invasion when law and order was established among the pagans.

Apparently not grasping the magnitude of the matter, Maggie opened another book from her pile.

Peter stood waiting as the clock ticked away. Yep, the library was closing as it always did, at exactly six o'clock. Not a minute earlier, and certainly not one minute later. This is not Italy, where nothing is on time. No, this is England, where clocks were invented at Greenwich. Weren't they? Well, certainly keeping proper time was!

She didn't want to keep him.

"I'll lock up when I leave," she warned.

"What?" Peter asked.

Was this woman provoking a revolution or something? What should be done? Peter wiped his brow and quickly rolled his cart off, wondering if the library had ever locked someone in all night? If they had, what did they have for supper? Surely the library got cold at night, as it typically was during the day. And then, can one really look at books on movie stars all night long? Peter was starting to get a headache after only a few words with this woman. It was soon to get much worse.

"So strange, that one," Maggie yammered to

Joan Crawford looking up at her with polished face and blackened eyelashes all perfectly arranged like picket fences around her eyes, which glistened with a "come-and-get-some" gleam.

Peter figured he could always inform Mrs. Woods that he never saw the young woman and only barely noticed her companion, Joan Crawford. Perhaps she slipped in after the bell chimed closing. Of course she did. *People from across the Channel are known to do strange things*, he thought. *Makes sense. Surely that's why most of them live over there.* Certainly, the English understood what the subtext "over there" meant.

It was raining all the way back to Mrs. Chapman's. Peter stood on the crowded tube train thinking about the creature with the red lips and wondering what would happen if she'd never left the library that evening. He was still thinking about this up in his room as he warmed a tin of soup on his electric two-burner plate that he was still making payments on—a payment always on time, every other week.

As the soup steamed, Peter pulled out his notebook to jot down a few more lines. How, he wondered, could he get it right in his novel when women were so obviously strange and wholly unpredictable? Nothing that woman at the library said, he thought, made any sense and yet every word she uttered was still jingling in his thoughts that night. Could she still be there? Sitting in that empty cold study hall with her red lips glowing in the dark as though there was an audience sitting silently below her gaze counting the moments until their rapture eclipsed their realities.

Peter ate his soup from the tin and sucked the last few drops when he realized it was nine o'clock—the time he always put his notebook down and crawled under his comforter. Through the thin walls, he could hear the couple in the other room making love. Her howls were compelling. Under his comforter, Peter wanked to the pleasing rhythm between the couple, with her moans and his jouncing the bed forming a nonverbal communication; well, lovers often communicate as if language has little to do with anything.

Jingle, jingle, jingle. Her words kept jingling in his thoughts. *How was she doing that?* Peter fell asleep wondering.

2

OVER THE DAYS that followed, Peter wondered what had happened to the woman with the red lips? His imagination took him to all kinds of places and scenarios. What if she had a secret life at the library where she had long conversations with movie stars, just as he secretly wrote lines in his novel about Scottish warriors and their ladyloves? What if?

Then, one night, as Peter was leaving for the day, there she was again, this time standing outside the library exit. Could she have just left from the day he encountered her the week before? *Things happen*, Peter reminded himself. *And no one knows why.*

"Hey, librarian. I nicked this book," the woman with the red lips confessed.

She waved a book in Peter's face. The other librarians looked at Maggie, and then at him.

"I may report you," he announced.

"Yep, but not likely. Know why?" she asked.

Peter paused to see what would come next.

"Cause you're a perv!" she announced and then looked at the others to gauge their reaction. "You spend all day at the library watching girls wearing tight sweaters."

Hers seemed to Peter to be particularly tight that night. Without again glimpsing at her tight sweater, he walked off.

But Maggie dashed after him and put her arm through his as though they were strolling down the mall to a picnic. Peter shook himself free.

"I'm Maggie. Fish and chips? I'm paying."

"What? Got to go home."

Somehow, even as he was still contemplating how she got her lips so red, he found himself standing next to her at a walk up stand with a plate of fish and chips in front of him. Things happen, you know?

"You're not one of those guys who live with their mum, are you?"

"Got a room at a house near Victoria station," Peter replied.

"One of those places where your girlfriend can't come up?" she asked.

"It's near Victoria," he repeated.

"Like what do you do when you're not squeezing a peek at me through those dusty ol' shelves?"

"Not squeezing… not looking at you," he stammered.

"Oh, you're looking at the dust between the books, hey?"

"I write."

"Write? Like what? Poetry?" she asked.

"No."

At the fish counter, Peter noticed how quickly men seemed to notice Maggie. Was it her sweater? She put a chip up to Peter's mouth and held it there until he finally parted his lips. *Where else could he go with this*, he wondered? Then she flipped it onto his tongue. He stood pondering what to do, but soon realized he was only staring at her lips. If he failed to chew, would she think he was trying to kiss her?

"Novel," he finally got out.

He went on chewing slowly, but not because he was concentrated on looking at her lips all the more. Well, maybe.

"You're writing a novel?"

"Yes."

"Me mum, she once said, 'Maggie, you may not get to be pretty enough to be no movie star. Plus, you don't got the money to get yourself to Hollywood anyway. Best write a novel then. It's your only hope out'."

"Write a novel? You ever read one?" Peter asked.

"No, but you see, if you're not a movie star, being a famous writer is almost the same. Sure, it is."

"How?" he wanted to know.

"Well, writers get piles of money, checks come in the post, you dress smart and go to parties at posh places. You know."

"No, I don't," he said, and meant it. "I don't go anywhere and don't want to go anywhere, do I?" He meant that in return.

"You're so peculiar," she said. "Are you sure you don't write dirty stories for dirty magazines? You look the type."

Maggie reached over and unbuttoned Peter's top shirt button. He quickly buttoned it back up again. Isn't it only Italian men who wear their shirts open because they have chest hair?

"What... ?"

Upon hearing her comment, he tossed his plate of soggy chips on the counter and walked off.

"So, peculiar. He's got to be a writer then!"

Joan Crawford may not have heard Maggie, but would surely have thought the same. It's told she knew more than a few writers in Hollywood and it's oft repeated that Joan knew them in a biblical sense. Joan would surely have said: 'Oh, well, things happen!"

* * *

At times, Peter woke up early, and to the sounds of the morning rains against his window, he'd scribble a few lines of his novel. Sometimes, the images that had stirred in his head at night kept him awake, and he wanted to write things out so he could understand the unfathomable, like Jamie, the Scottish warrior who loved Claire but couldn't truly be a warrior if he got too mushy over her. Could he? But then, things happen. Peter looked forward to reading a few more pages of the *Outlander* at the library to see what the author might reveal. With those meandering thoughts, he dressed, grabbed his handwritten manuscript, and headed downstairs, where Mrs. Chapman was sure to greet him with her warm smile.

"Here's your toast, Peter. Didn't sleep well last night?"

Peter patted down his unruly, wavy dark hair, and answered with a smile.

"Six more pages for your daughter to type. I just finished them this morning. Here's some money for her, too."

He put a coin on the table and sat down to gobble his toast and slurp his tea.

"Alice says she won't take money. She so enjoys reading your words."

"I have to pay her."

"She said you only made one spelling error in all those pages she typed last week," Mrs. Chapman added.

"That's good, Mrs. Chapman. Got to go."

Peter stuffed the last of his toast into his mouth and dashed as he was never late to work. But then again, he was never early either.

The working day at the library was good. Mrs. Woods was too busy to see if Peter was shelving his books or merely riding the aisles, pausing here and there to add to his novel. It didn't seem long before it was six o'clock. Luckily, the rain had stopped late that afternoon. Peter could walk back to

Mrs. Chapman's to save the tube fare. He grabbed his notebook, slid it under his jacket, and headed for the door, where he followed Mrs. Woods outside.

And there she was again—the woman with the red lips.

"Here I am!" she screeched to Mrs. Woods as though a surrendering criminal.

Mrs. Woods jumped in her tracks.

"Petey said he would report me to the King. You see, I nicked this book!"

Maggie waved a library book at Mrs. Woods.

"Peter. My name is Peter," he said under his breath.

Mrs. Woods took the book, and opening it, looked at Maggie as if she was missing her senses.

"Miss, your book is not due till next week. Perhaps you should drop a note to the King informing him of such. Given the gravity of the situation, it will most certainly ease his mind."

Mrs. Woods handed the book back and walked off.

"Why did you do that?" Peter asked.

"How should I know?" Maggie replied. "Sometimes it all comes out wrong. Hey, I got my dole money. I'm treating you to a proper meal for saving me from being shipped off to Australia. That's where they send book nickers."

"No, they don't. I got to get home."

Peter left Maggie standing with her near-to-being overdue book. Still, she caught up with him. Things can happen when you're least expecting them. In fact, at times they simply jump out at you.

"I'm Maggie."

"I remember your name," he mused. "You didn't remember mine."

She slid her arm through his as she had the week before, but Peter pulled away just as quickly. He wondered what

Mrs. Woods would think had she seen him walk off with this strange creature? Perhaps that he was part of a crime dual that purposely, and with deliberate intent, held books out of circulation until they were near to being overdue?

It was a crowded pub that Maggie dragged Peter to, never once releasing her clutch along the way.

There was a fireplace near the table where they were seated. Peter didn't notice the glowing fire; he only noticed the prices on the menu and wondered what the waiter would think if he only ordered a glass of water. Shortly after, the waiter appeared with a bottle of wine and two glasses, but Peter was not tempted.

"Oh, no. I don't drink," he informed the waiter.

Still Maggie had other thoughts and frequently did.

"Yes, two glasses," she shot back.

The waiter poured two glasses of wine and left the bottle on the table.

A whole bottle? But how much did it cost? Peter wondered, and *if they still had debtors' prisons in London?*

"You in London during the blitz?" she asked.

"Yeah. My dad, he wouldn't leave our house. Mum, she wouldn't go anywhere without him. The night the bombs hit, there was nothing left of my folks."

"Where were you," she asked.

"Mum always made me go to the shelter. Packed me a sandwich every night. Told me to pray for them."

"Did you?" she asked. "Pray for them?"

"Couldn't figure out who to pray to," Peter replied. "You?"

"Me mum went to live with her sister in Cornwall," she said. "I stayed in London. Had a job at the phone company. Lied about my age to get it. Yep, plugged in wires all damned day. I did. Plugged one in for Churchill once. Can you believe?"

He could. Things happen.

"Your mum?" he asked as he took the first sip of his wine.

"Yeah, we live together. Probably always will."

"What about your dad?"

"Long gone," Maggie said. "Mum only says 'here today, gone tomorrow like the leftovers.' Who cares anyway? Things like that never last, do they?"

"Like what? You mean he left you? You and your mum?"

"I never knew what happened. That strange?" she said.

"I guess," Peter replied.

"Maybe he got on a bus and went the wrong way and never came back. You got a girlfriend?"

Peter shifted in his seat uncomfortably.

"Oh, it don't matter. The men I know, they all chase skirts at work and stay out nights trying to get under one. But you, you're special."

"Special?" he asked, and then felt compelled to take a second sip of wine. "No, not special. Work at the library."

"But you're writing a novel. A real novel."

Maggie gulped the rest of her wine and poured a second glass. She started to refill Peter's glass, but it was still near to being full.

"You read? I mean novels?" he asked.

Maggie was uncomfortable with this question and gazed into fire.

"Petey, I never tell people, but I can't read or write. Well, no more than my name and address, I guess."

"But I often see you at the library reading stacks of books."

"Not reading. Just looking at the pictures of movie stars. You see, I had to go out and work when I was a kid. Me and Mum, we cleaned houses. Never went to school. When a truant officer sent a letter asking about me we just packed for a new address. Moved a lot back then. Yeah, but maybe it was because we couldn't make rent. Don't know."

Maggie put down her glass. Her sadness seemed to evaporated with her smile.

"Yeah, right… Huh? There's always a new day, hey?"

For the first time, Peter and Maggie's eyes wandered into each other's even as the conversation went silent. It seemed as though there was a silent communication between them. He could feel it, and wondered if she did, too. But did he like that feeling? Were his knees a bit weak? He reached down and grabbed his knee to see. But nothing was shaking. Not that much anyway. Warrior Jamie Fraser would have been impressed.

During supper the light from the fire danced across Peter's features and made his wavy dark hair appear shiny. Maggie smiled and went on, but there was a sadness in her eyes and her voice become soft as though she was revealing things she'd kept hidden back.

"Petey, you know me mum, she was real pretty once. Yeah, she was. But look what it did for her…"

"What do you mean?" he asked.

Maggie took another sip of wine and paused before continuing.

"Well, she sure ain't no movie star, is she?" Maggie declared defiantly. "Never even met man who'd take the time to look past her pretty face. But Petey, a pretty face, it don't last long when you're down on your knees scrubbing floors. I can see it in my Mum's eyes."

"See what?"

"A sadness. Even when she's smiling. You know? She feels worn out, is what I mean."

"You really want to be a movie star?" he asked.

Movie stars seemed so far away to Peter, but then he recalled his mum once saying that Laurence Olivier and Vivien Leigh had a country house just outside of London. It seems they were always there when they weren't making films in America.

"Don't know really," she said. "I guess I just don't want to end up like me mum. Maybe nothing scares me more. I look at her and I know that's gonna be me one day, sooner or later. Nothing but a worn-out cleaning rag ain't nobody gonna care about!"

"But who knows what that 'later' will be like, I mean, until we get there?" he asked, and in the flash of the moment, wondered how Claire and Jamie saw into their own futures. But what if they were still looking? Looking for each other in some other place and time that was yet to come for them. Yet, isn't that the way it is for all lovers? Peter never stopped pondering those imponderables he collected in his thoughts.

"Easy for you. You're a man," she said. "It don't matter how pretty you are unless you want to be a movie star. Hey? Don't you think Tyrone Power is the most beautiful man in the world?"

"Never thought about it. I mean, I guess," Peter answered.

All the way home, Peter thought about what Maggie had said. About how things were for women after they'd lost their beauty; that is, if they started out with it. Perhaps it was easier for women who weren't pretty. Peter thought himself lucky he didn't really worry about his looks. Well, except when he was glued to the mirror, wondering if anything looked different than the day before, what with the curls in his hair never heading the same direction after waking.

3

M RS. CHAPMAN HAD KNOWN Peter since the war. She and her daughter met him in the air raid shelters, which, for their district, was deep below the Victoria tube. Come dusk, everyone scrambled below ground, knowing that sooner or later, the bombers would come in waves. They all tried to put their best faces on in the knowledge that the night could be the one that leveled their home and put them living on a street of ruble.

Down in the near-darkness, people sang in a big chorus, loud enough so that the bombers might think they were so fearless they'd know it would be pointless to return the next night. But the bombers came anyway and did so in waves. One of the few houses spared in that district was Mrs. Chapman's, where her daughter had been raised. Life had not been easy for them before the war, and only the fact that their house survived the blitz enabled them to get on. You see, Mrs. Chapman had a few extra rooms she could let to make ends meet. She and Alice shared the maid's room off the kitchen and had boarders in the rooms upstairs. The house had been, back in the day, the home of a shop-keeper, and he displayed his prosperity by having a live-in maid. Now, Mrs. Chapman was the maid, did the cleaning, and prepared meals for some of the boarders while Alice kept an office job. They both worked hard to keep things going and felt so much more blessed than those, like Peter's folks, who had no place to go home to after the bombers came.

There in the dark of the shelter, Mrs. Chapman would chat to Peter as Alice slept with her head on her mum's lap. At times, Peter was afraid, and seemed to know that the day would come, and he'd have no place to call home. The war wasn't over when Peter moved into Mrs. Chapman's. Soon, he was working at the library as he felt the need to always be surrounded by words; those mysterious devices that can easily convey one to far off places without a ticket or even the means to buy one.

Peter had worked at the library for some time before the woman with the movie star lips seemed to glide into his life. Perhaps the way movie stars drift into the daydreams of the worshipful.

During the winter days, after Peter first saw the woman with the red lips, he shelved his books, and when Mrs. Woods wasn't looking, read from the *Outlander*, or wrote a few more lines in his novel. The time passed quickly, and before he thought about it much, it was already six o'clock. Life was fairly predictable. His only concern most days was whether to splash out on a tube fare or walk and save his money. Well, the habits of wartime economies don't fall off easily.

Back at Mrs. Chapman's, Peter had just put down his notebook and unbuttoned his shirt when there was a tap at his door. He quickly buttoned back up and went to answer.

"Peter, did you forget?" Mrs. Chapman asked.

"Forget?"

He checked his top button. No, everything was in order.

"You're eating with us. Alice has a nice pie. Apple, I think.

Peter smiled and nodded.

"I'll be right down."

He closed the door to check the mirror. His wavy hair was mostly in order, as much as it ever was, so he headed downstairs to the kitchen, delighted that he didn't have to eat tinned soup that night.

Alice was placing the plates on the table when Peter came in. She greeted him with a bright smile. She always smiled when she saw Peter. There was a glint in her pretty brown eyes that always made him want to smile back.

Mrs. Chapman showed Peter the apple pie. It was a treat as, during the war, sugar was rationed and few had puddings of any kind.

"Peter, your writing is so lyrical. I could read your pages over and over," Alice remarked.

She smiled again at him. Mrs. Chapman smiled, too, which made Peter think of how much alike they looked.

"Yeah?" he responded and took a seat.

"Like when Tom takes Pippa's hand—she pulls back but he takes it again and kisses it. You write that she's never been kissed before. Can't imagine how it felt. When will you start looking for an agent?"

Peter looked puzzled.

"Agent?"

"All novelist have an agent so they don't get cheated by the publisher."

"Don't know," he replied. "I guess. One day, I mean."

"Peter's not yet finished. Are you, dear?" Mrs. Chapman asked and sat down as Alice passed him a plate of pot roast.

For the rest of the supper, Alice talked about the novel, which had carried her along on a journey to another time, place, and love. To Peter, it seemed as though she loved his words so much she'd memorized them. *How much will women love his novel*, he wondered as the question settled into his dreams of the future.

The next day, Peter was in such a good mood that he thought about sleeping in a bit, but then he was never late, so he got up and went over to the mirror to see which way his curls had settled. If they fell the way he felt looked best, he thought it predicted a good day ahead.

On the way to the library, Peter wondered if Maggie would be there. After all, there's only so many pictures of movie stars one can look at, and then what? Well, perhaps movie stars fade into the fantasies we conjure after the lights go down and dwell there with us forever. What if…?

Peter's cart of books seemed to pull him towards the table she typically sat. He wanted to look at her from hiding as if he might somehow come by a few clues that explained her strangeness. Maybe the kind the vulnerable frequently swaddle themselves so no one expects them to conform in a world that they suspect will reject them all the same.

Peter smiled. Yes, there she was again, her head deep in a big book. The title was printed large and read "Hollywood Legends." He pondered how this creature could be so enthralled by the black and white images that she never noticed him peeking between the books. But that's not what happened. No, things happen other than as we might expect, and that can be confounding. Even without looking his way, she motioned for him to approach with her finger. Come here, it beckoned. But could that mean women can see through books as they seem to see through men? Peter rolled his cart around the racks to where she was sitting. The library table lamp flickered and then went out. The dim light hanging above made her cheekbones look, well, like Joan Crawford's.

"Is it?"

"Is what it?" he asked.

Still she didn't look up.

"In case you're wondering," she finally said, "it's not six o'clock. But it could still happen."

"What? What could happen?" he asked.

Why was this creature so unsettling? Peter wondered.

"I want you to read your novel to me," she announced.

"Why?"

No one had asked him to read the novel, but then again, only Mrs. Chapman and Alice knew he was writing one.

"Why? she asked. "Because I want to be the first to know what happens."

"Happens?"

"Something always happens in novels. Something real pretty does, even if it never does in real life."

"I can't read my novel in the library," he informed her in his official librarian voice that would surely have impressed

Mrs. Woods.

"I know. Reading's not permitted in the library."

Peter could only wonder what this woman was talking about as nothing she ever said seemed to make sense. Or at least not the kind of bottled up sense he was comfortable in. There was a long pause as Peter put his thoughts in order.

"Read…?" He all but stammered.

"Come by on Sunday," she said. "Mum will cook, and you can read to us."

"I have to work Sunday," Peter informed her. His mouth couldn't come up with anything else. His gaze locked on her as if his eyes didn't want to move on, or perhaps he didn't want them to.

"The Library is closed," she said and flipped the page to Carol Lombard, who smiled up at Maggie as though she'd long been waiting to chat.

"It is? Nobody ever told me that," he replied.

"You stand outside the library on Sundays waiting for it not to open, hey?"

"No. I was kidding… Sort of. I work on my novel Sundays."

"Number Seven, Baker Street. Just down from Victoria Station. Six o'clock. You can remember six o'clock because you go around telling everyone it's six o'clock all the time."

"What? No, I don't!" he said. "Only when the library is closing."

"It's Sunday. It's not open."

"Of course, I know that. I'll come… at six."

"Why are you always so difficult?" Maggie demanded.

"What? Me, you say?"

"I think your books are way overdue!" she said before slamming her book closed and walking off.

Peter yelled after her loud enough for the library patrons to shush him.

"No, they're not!"

Peter checked his top shirt button. But only he had come undone.

"I've never had an overdue book!"

Well, who would have thought otherwise?

4

PETER LEFT EARLY for supper at Maggie's because he's never late, but he had problems finding Number Seven. Knowing how deliberately perplexing this woman was, he presumed she had most likely moved the house to another number just to confound him, and then he'd be late for supper. Peter was never, ever late. Would she do something like that? He asked a passerby where her place was. She knew where Maggie lived and pointed to the right building.

Maggie's mum answered the door.

"Come in. You're the near-to-being famous writer that Mags is always talking about," she said. "And she never let on that you're as cute as they come!"

"Me? Not cute, I work at the library," Peter said denying his cuteness. Because didn't he rely on the man in mirror by his door to remind him that he wasn't all that cute? They met to exchange glances every morning at exactly the same time.

Mary ushered him to the kitchen where pots were steaming and chops frying. The table was set with different sizes of plates painted with flowers and such. Peter looked them over to see if any matched. None did, except in their unique floral borders.

"You noticed my plates? Every time one of the neighbors move, they end up giving me a plate or two. I think I have nearly a dozen now. Aren't they pretty? Told Mags I'd give them to her when she got married."

"What did she say?" Peter asked.

"Oh, I guess she don't care about my plates," Mary said. "Don't know if it's because they're not posh enough, or she thinks I want her to settle down and, well, you know?"

But he didn't.

Moments later, Maggie swept in like she was

Loretta Young making her grand entrance on her television show. Peter wondered if she was late coming to the table because it had taken her so long to put that many coats of lipstick on. Is that possible?

"Peter, you found us?" Some people don't, you know?" Was this a confession of sorts? "Because it's not really Number Seven here, is it, Mum? It's Number Seventeen, but someone nicked the "one," so the post would never get his bills to the right address."

Peter wondered why he expected Maggie to say such a thing. Because she was a self-confessed book nicker? You see, by the same token, Peter thought, they would never get a letter from the library informing them their book was overdue.

Soon after they sat down to eat, Peter felt the women watching his every move. He slowly lifted his fork towards his mouth. They paused to see what would happen next. Before he'd taken his second bite, Mary was planning the second.

"Have another chop, Peter." Mary forked one over to his plate, where it dropped on the one he'd barely taken his first bite from.

"Yes, Mrs…" was all he could get out.

"Call me Mary."

"That was my mum's name," Peter mused as he'd just been thinking that Mary was as warm and soft-spoken as his mum.

"Oh, how sweet," Mary said. "Huh, Mags?"

"Nothing sweet about it. Just a coincidence," Maggie demurred.

"Don't mind her. She only sees things through a block of ice!"

"That ain't never gonna melt!" Maggie replied.

As soon as Peter's last fork of food reached his mouth Mary went for the dessert plates as Maggie cleared away the dishes for his reading.

"Oh, I have cake, Peter," Mary said. "Got it with my rations. Can you believe the war's been over this long and we're still clipping rationing coupons?"

"Mum and Churchill were the only ones certain we'd win. The rest of us were learning German and trying to swallow a lot of sauerkraut to see if we could keep it down."

Mary put a big piece of cake on a plate and handed it to Peter with a wink as if it was his birthday. He smiled. It was the kind of happy moment that reminded him of his folks.

"So, now it's time for Petey's novel," Maggie announced the moment Peter put down his dessert fork after the last bite of cake.

"Can't wait! I'll turn out the lights. It'a be like the cinema."

"Mum, how's he going to read in the dark?" Maggie complained.

"I'll light a candle," Mary said.

Mary went over to the cabinet and pulled out a tall church candle in a jar, lit it, and placed it in front of Peter.

"Had this during the war when we had to put the lights out," Mary said.

"And light all the candles we could find so the bombers would think we were in church and wouldn't bomb us. Right, Mum?" Maggie added.

Mary waved Maggie off and Peter opened his manuscript to the pages that Alice had typed only that week, and began reading by candlelight. The flickering light seemed to dance over their faces as it does when movie stars look down at us from the silver screen and see their aura reflected from the smiling faces below.

"Then, she heard pebbles tossed at her window," Peter read. "She knew he would come, despite everything that had come between them. She dashed from her bed to open the window. But it wasn't him. It was the man that never in her dreams did she expect to see again. At that moment she realized that she'd never lost her love for him. Across the room flooded with moonlight, he carried her back to her bed in silence. One that would endure the rest of the night for them…"

As Mary dabbed tears from her eyes, Maggie looked lost in the moment. Peter closed his manuscript. He could see that these women were taken by his story.

"That's nearly the end of the last part," he said to break the silence.

"I know you're going to be a big star!" Mary announced.

"He's a writer, Mum, not a film star," Maggie, the ice queen said.

"Oh, what's the difference? Who's ever heard of you?"

"Don't you think Petey looks like Tyrone Power?" Maggie stood behind his chair weaving her fingers through his hair.

"Well, I think he looks more like Errol Flynn," Mary said, "when he was Robin Hood and lived in Nottingham Forest. That's not far from us, huh, Mags?"

"No, Mum. It's just around the corner where all the movie stars live."

"Ice, like I told you, Peter. That's my Maggie."

Maggie mussed Peter's wavy hair pushing the part to the other side.

"See, if he parted his hair like this, he'd look just like Errol Flynn."

Mary was delighted and clapped as Maggie gave Peter a big kiss on the cheek, which left a spot of lipstick.

"Lipstick! Now everyone will know you have a girlfriend."

Peter smiled contentedly. He was in rapture from all the attention these women had lavished on him.

"Peter, you must be hungry. Another piece of chocolate cake?" Mary asked. Her voice echoed that of Peter's own mum from some chamber of his recollections. He smiled at the thought.

5

Post-war London was a tough place for two unmarried women like Maggie and her mum to get by. Things were still rationed as in the war; jobs were scarce and paid miserable wages. Their survival depended on Maggie finding work and keeping it. But things didn't always work out. Still, they did what they could.

After walking up and down High Street for what seemed like days on end, Maggie finally found a job doing what she did best—trying on lipstick and looking at the results in the mirror. Joan Crawford would have understood. She, too, was good with lipstick.

Selfridges was a tony store that served a well-heeled clientele. Maggie had applied for jobs several times, but the fact that she couldn't read or write limited the positions she might hold. By making herself look like a movie star, she'd convinced them that a position at the makeup counter was a good move. She was right. Well, sort of.

Ann, a pretty young lady, all makeup counter girls were pretty, got her started by unpacking boxes and lining up the fancy goods on the glass shelves behind the counter.

"Now, make sure the rows are perfectly straight.

Miss Livingston can spot a box, not just right all the way from the mezzanine. That's where she spies on us to see if we're talking too much."

But Maggie was already bored.

"Oh, never mind her. Where's the loo?" Maggie asked.

"You can't go to the loo until lunch," Ann announced.

"Watch me. I can find a loo with or without a map! It's true. They're never more than one or two escalator rides away. And think about all the pretty things we'll see on the way! Follow me, I'll show you."

Maggie patted Ann on the head.

"Don't worry. We'll be back soon after lunch."

Ann didn't know what to say.

"And leave the counter without a girl?"

She shook her head and went back to putting the new merchandise out. Maggie headed for her destination, which took in a bit of window shopping along the way.

After nearly an hour had passed, Ann became anxious as she'd been assigned the task of breaking in the new girl. Then, Ann caught sight of "Bulldog," as they called head floorwalker Livingston, slowly making her way towards Ann's counter.

"Oh, Miss Livingston."

Ann couldn't think of anything else to say to her boss.

About then Maggie came sashaying down the aisle as though she'd never been anywhere. Livingston did a double take.

"I'm Maggie."

"Yes, the new girl. I saw your lips coming before I could make out the face."

Miss Livingston handed Maggie a tissue.

"Here, blot 'em down. Our customers are not tarts," she announced.

"Might be more interesting if they were!" Maggie quipped.

She winked at Ann who moved away from the new girl as though she'd just been confirmed a leper.

"This is your first day here, Miss. Could easily be your last," Livingston said, as if she'd been trained by Churchill to lead the troops over the Channel. Not expecting anything but total capitulation, Livingston continued on her morning rounds. Well, she didn't know Maggie.

"Here, put these in neat rows up there," Ann said. "And watch your mouth. Livingston will fire you before the week's out."

"Nah. I'll get around her," Maggie replied.

How she'd do that was yet to be determined. Maybe she'd just plug her nose until she passed out. Hadn't it worked at the library? Well, that one was still up for grabs.

About then, a fashionably dressed customer approached.

"Miss, what is the most popular shade of lipstick these days?" she asked Maggie. "There are so many to choose from now that the war is over."

Maggie grabbed the closest tube and waved it in the customer's face as though it were a magic wand.

"Well, the one the tarts love is this Bloody Raspberry Delight. It sure enough is, isn't it, Ann?"

The customer's mouth fell open. Ann cringed as Selfridges was hardly a place where streetwalkers shopped. Courtesans perhaps, but surely not streetwalkers.

"Tarts? Did you say tarts, Miss?

"Yeah, the whores down in Soho."

Maggie winked as if they both surely knew what she was talking about.

Ann quickly jumped in to rescue the moment.

"She means 'Raspberry Delight,' Madam. She's new here."

Maggie tended to see things in unconventional ways. She leaned over the counter to give the customer an example.

"It's a big secret," she said and looked around should others overhear. "We can't keep enough of this in stock. You know how men like us to be exciting and how, during the war, we had to sell our souls for a bit of lipstick?"

"You're right," the customer replied. "My husband said he was tired of my cooking. But I think he's really bored with me! I'll take six of the…"

"Bloody Raspberry Delight. Best take a dozen; as you know, we'll be sold out before closing. Won't we, Ann?"

"Yes. Two dozen. I want to help my neighbor save her marriage, too. Put it on my account," the woman said. "It will be a Christmas present to myself."

"Be a dear, and write this up," Maggie asked Ann. "I'll wrap them up straight away."

As Ann wrote up the sale, Maggie wrapped the lipstick in tissue and handed the purchase to the delighted customer, who walked off smiling.

"Here's your sales book," Ann said.

Maggie tossed it on the counter with indifference. Still, a sale of two dozen tubes was more than anyone else typically made in a day, maybe even a week. Maggie knew she was in the running, although she was yet not sure where she was running to. But as it was, she had nowhere else to go anyway. The big sale couldn't have been better timed as about then Miss Livingston reappeared. She grabbed Maggie's sales book off the counter and glanced at the entries.

"Your sales are impressive, Miss. Particularly in lipstick, it would seem."

"I'm very good with lipstick. You see, my boyfriend is a famous writer. He takes me to posh places where I have to look, well, posh. And I never blot!"

Miss Livingston, who'd heard every imaginable story from her girls, seemed skeptical.

"I see," she said. "All the same, keep it up."

She marched off, but then turned to grab an eyeful of her two counter girls. She could only wonder what they had up their nicely pressed sleeves that day.

"I told you I'd get around her," Maggie announced.

"Posh places, hey?" Ann said. "You said your boyfriend worked at a library. That ain't 'posh' in my book."

"Yeah, but what's the difference? Books are books, except in yours, I guess."

Maggie reached for a tube of Raspberry Delight and applied a few more coats. Joan Crawford was surely smiling down from the celluloid heavens.

Peter's days ran about the same speed no matter what. Maybe about as fast as an organ grinder's. He worked at the library from nine until precisely six, went home, gulped down his tin of soup, and then jotted a few lines in his novel before tucking in. Only on Saturday did he wander about Notting Hill doing his marketing. He avoided actually going into stores unless he had to for fear there could be lurking forces that might separate him from his money. It was a particularly sunny day when Peter was out buying tins of soup for the week when he ran into Alice. She was happy to see him. Alice was always glad to see Peter.

"Oh, Peter!" she yelled from across the street.

Peter waved and went over to chat.

"Hi, Alice. What are you up to?"

"Just finished marketing. Come down for supper. Just me and Mum and one of her shepherd's pie."

"Sure. I've eaten tinned soup all week. I'll come down. What time?"

"Seven?"

"Great, thanks Alice."

Peter took her bag of groceries and they headed back to Mrs. Chapman's.

"You're nearly finished, aren't you?" she asked.

"Don't know for sure. Seems like the characters always have more to say."

"Remember, when you're finished, you'll have to decide on an agent."

"Yeah, but I don't know one."

"Did you forget? I work for one. Come talk to Fred when you're finished."

"You're so good to me, typing my novel and all."

"You're going to be a great writer one day, I just know it. Most of the manuscripts Fred gets aren't worth burning."

"Yeah? You really think I'm good?"

"Yes, and when you're finished, I'll put your novel at the top of Fred's pile to read. I will, too!"

6

MAGGIE AND ANN got on well at the cosmetics counter. They worked hard, at least when it was likely Livingston might be looking down from the mezzanine, and then had a few laughs to make the time chimed when their 'Bulldog' boss was on her rounds.

"How's your famous writer boyfriend?" Ann asked.

"You laugh, but wait and see! I'll show them all up!" Maggie replied.

But what was Maggie going to show and to whom was still uncharted territory. It would get tangled!

"Yeah, I know all about it," Ann declared. "My last boyfriend was a famous singer, or at least in his mind he was."

"Petey's different," Maggie said and pulled out a mirror to check her makeup.

"Artists are all different. Sure, they are," Ann remarked. "They get their girlfriends to pay their bills because, you know, they're 'different' and don't have bills because they never open their mail. Someone else takes care of that, like us!"

"Here, Madam. Why don't we try our new shade of lipstick on you?"

Maggie pulled out a tube of lipstick and drew red target circles on Ann's face. They laughed until they saw Livingston heading their way.

"Duck! There's Bulldog Livingston!"

Ann ducked down before the 'bulldog' made her way through the customers and reached the counter.

"Where's Ann?" she asked. "Didn't I just see her?"

"Oh, Ann got sick," Maggie declared with a straight face. "Puking up a storm, that one. You know how it is; too much to drink last night, what with that rowdy boyfriend of hers. He's a famous singer, you know?"

Livingston had quickly come to terms with the fact that not much that came out of Maggie's mouth was of benefit and walked off without commenting.

But certainly, Ann had heard Maggie. Stooped down behind the counter, she pulled off her heeled shoe and walloped Maggie's foot soundly. Then did it again for good measure. She shrieked from the pain. Hearing it, Miss Livingston did an about face, but Maggie simply flashed her a benign smile.

Miss Livingston walked on. There were more important battles to face that day.

"She's gone!"

Ann picked up a mirror to find smeared red circles on her face.

"I really don't think I care for this shade, Miss," she said.

"I heard you the first time," Maggie announced, and grabbed her throbbing foot.

* * *

There were times late in the wee hours, when Peter simply got so lost in his writing that all other worlds seemed to disappear from thought. It was easy for him to live in the characters he'd painted with words. Even the couple jouncing the bed in the next room didn't grab his attention that night.

"Last four pages. I'm finished! Finished!"

With that declaration of victory, he jumped into bed, turned the light out, and pulled the comforter up. It was a cold night and he wondered if the Scots warrior Jamie and Clare were thinking of one another. Maybe longing for a caress, or perhaps even more.

The next morning, with a big grin on his face, Peter headed

downstairs for breakfast. Down in her kitchen, Mrs. Chapman had heard him stirring and had his toast ready.

"Mrs. Chapman, I'm done!" he proclaimed.

He handed those precious last pages of his novel manuscript to her.

"Oh, Peter, I'm so proud of you," she said. "I'll give your papers to Alice. She can type them this week, and then you're off to fame and fortune."

"Just getting it published is my dream," he said. "Guess I don't really think about fame or fortune, do I?"

With a smile, Peter grabbed his toast and headed to the door. Yes, he was riding high that morning.

That day, Peter didn't mind pushing his cart from aisle to aisle as he was sure he'd soon be going from writer to published novelist. It was a long dream that was near to being a reality. All those hours he'd spent writing and not doing much else was going to pay off. *Soon*, he thought. But things happen, and often in ways one could never, ever have expected.

Peter was in such an up mood he decided to walk to the library that morning. Did he look to be brimming with happiness, or were people smiling back at him because the sun was so brilliant for everyone?

Just before lunch, Mrs. Woods walked by and, as always, glanced at the books piled high on his cart. This time, Peter didn't run for cover. No, he gave her a big smile. She walked on, but then wondered what Peter had going, and glanced back only to get another big smile. She turned, and whispered to herself.

"Ah, he's finished his novel,"

Peter was eager to see Maggie that day. She typically strolled in late afternoons after she left the store. But Maggie was already sitting at the big library table by the time he rolled his cart that way. This time, Peter didn't peek through the books at her, and instead stood by the study table saying nothing. His brilliant smile was enough.

"What?" she asked. "Oh, you're finished! Are you? Finished?"

"Finished! Want to celebrate?"

Maggie smiled, jumped up, looked around should someone see, and then kissed Peter on the mouth.

That evening, when Peter was off, they walked arm in arm like any couple. It felt almost like Christmas. Yep, in Peter's every thought the lights were twinkling bright.

"Think about it…" she said.

"I'm thinking. But about what?" he asked.

"We'll be going to posh parties about this time next month or the month after, hey?"

"Alice hasn't finished typing the last pages yet. Then I guess I have to send it to an agent."

"Who are you going to send it to?" Maggie asked.

"Why are you always walking me down streets before I've yet reached the crosswalk?" Peter wondered.

"What? I'm walking us towards a plate of food. Close your eyes and you can smell it from just over the crossing. Can you?" she asked. "Pasta with tomato sauce and lots of cheese. On the other side of the street over there. Let's go."

She paused only to begin kissing him all over his face. He wasn't in any hurry for her to stop.

"Yikes, I got a bit of lipstick on your mouth."

And he felt it to the tips of his curled-up toes. Peter was flying high that night.

* * *

The next evening, when Peter returned to Mrs. Chapman's, he'd brought a tin of corned beef. He wanted to celebrate and had stopped at the corner grocery on his way home from the library.

"Look, Alice, Peter brought a tin of corned beef. I haven't seen a tin this size since before the war! Are we celebrating?"

"I'm almost finished typing. On the last page, in fact," Alice announced.

"Thanks, Alice. Must owe you nearly a pound."

"I love being a tiny part of your big novel," she said.

Before long and a cup of tea or two, Mrs. Chapman placed a platter of corned beef surrounded by potatoes on the table and motioned for Peter to take a seat.

"So, novelist, what's the next step?" she asked.

"I asked my girlfriend if she'd post my manuscript to your boss on her way work."

Alice looked crestfallen when Peter mentioned "girlfriend," as did her mum, as there simply weren't that many good men out there, let alone one as cute as Peter, who'd long seemed like family. So, was he taken?

"I could have taken it in, Peter," Alice said but seemed to stumble over the words.

"Girlfriend?" Mrs. Chapman asked, shooting a glance Alice's way. "You never said anything about a girlfriend."

"She calls me her boyfriend. As things go, I guess that makes her my girlfriend. Yes?"

Peter's beaming smile said it all, and so much more. It was obvious he was in love. But Alice wasn't smiling. She put her fork down as she'd suddenly lost her appetite. Yep, her heart had sunk to the very bottom of her secret dreams.

At the agency the next day, Alice wasn't in any better mood. She sat at her desk, gloomily going through the manuscripts writers had sent. Fred noticed how forlorn she appeared. Well, reading piles of mostly the same stuff that came in the post would make anyone blue.

"Alice, I know how these manuscripts are depressing. Awful writing, awful, awful. Is that it?"

"Oh, they're not so bad," Alice replied, albeit looking a bit morose. "I mean some of them are... No, you're right, they're mostly awful."

Alice seemed to only sink deeper as she looked over the stack of manuscripts she faced having to read that morning.

"Something bothering you?" Fred asked.

In frustration, she shoved the pile of manuscripts back and forth over her desk as though she was looking for something that never happened.

"What if you found the greatest novel you'd ever read, and it was right there all along? Something you'd been waiting for all your life, but he got away?"

"He, you say?" Fred asked. "He did?"

"I mean 'it' got way. It did. Never even seemed to notice me. I mean not really notice."

Fred was perplexed trying to parse Alice's angst-filled philosophical question.

"And went on to be the best-selling novel ever, huh?" he asked.

"Sort of like that, I guess," she said. "Yeah, like that."

"Me, if I'd missed the best seller of the decade, I reckon I'd will myself over to the embankment and drop myself into that dirty river," Fred said. "At least I might if it wasn't too cold that day. I hate cold water, you know."

Fred's comment about ending it all by hurling himself into the Thames hardly lifted Alice's mood. But then she understood he'd jump only on a day when the waters were warm, but as they never were, Fred seemed saved. But not so Alice.

"Yeah? So that's how I feel," she said.

"I've got to read this one."

Fred took the manuscript Alice was struggling with and headed back to his office.

It was all Alice could do to keep from crying.

7

MAGGIE WAS LATE to Selfridges that Wednesday, but then she was mostly always late period. Ann was stocking the shelves when Maggie dashed behind the counter all ready to appear busy. She was good at make-believe, that is looking as though she'd been there all along. Isn't that how movie stars did it? Make-believe they were really some other person in some other place in time that stood still for them?

"Miss Livingston in? Need to do some shopping," she announced.

"She's on her rounds," Ann replied. "You've barely got here and you're already planning your escape?"

"I've got to find a new shirt for Petey. It's kind of an act of mercy, you know. So, don't you think Bulldog should let me off for that?"

"Doesn't he have closets full of shirts? I mean like all famous writ-ers?" Ann asked.

"He has an empty closet because the only shirt he has is hanging on his back. What floor are men's shirts?"

"I know how many coins you have to your name, so, try the bargain basement. It's in the basement," Ann said sarcastically.

Maggie looked around to see if she could spot Bulldog Livingston.

"What floor is that again?" Maggie asked with a smirk.

"Three," Ann replied. "They moved the basement up to three just to confuse bargain hunters. Just take the up escalator and you'll end up there."

"I'll just jump. It's faster!"

With a smile, Maggie headed down to the basement to find Peter a new shirt.

* * *

Things weren't going well for Alice, and therefore,

Mrs. Chapman was no better. The news that darling Peter had a girlfriend hadn't set well.

Mrs. Chapman was catching up on her ironing as a pot of soup simmered when Alice came in.

"How's Peter's typing coming along?" she asked her daughter.

"Finished." Alice said. "Do you think Peter will move on when he becomes published?"

Alice stopped stirring the soup and fell into a chair, looking glum.

"Dear, you tell Peter how much you love his writing,"

Mrs. Chapman began.

"And I do…" Alice's voice was filled with angst.

"But when did you ever tell him how much you like him?"

"You ever tell a man you loved him?" Alice asked.

"Only your dad."

"When?" Alice asked.

"Well, had to be the day after he ran off with that woman. Dear, Peter isn't going to ask you out unless he knows you're interested in him. Men hate rejection, you know."

"Mum, are you burning that hole in my blouse purposely?"

"What? Oh, no, dear. This one's an accident, so think nothing of it."

Alice grabbed her blouse to see two burned holes.

"Mum!" she screeched.

"What? Is my sauce burning? I knew something was!"

* * *

On her day off, Maggie mostly wandered around looking into shop windows waiting until the library would open. She was eager to give Peter his new shirt, but then wondered if he would appreciate the gesture. After all, there had to be some reason why he wore the same drab gray shirt day in and day out. But how do you ask a man why, particularly if you've never met one who wore the same shirt every day. To Maggie, Peter was simply peculiar and certainly not like the men she'd known. In that regard, it made him unique. Yep, maybe even grounded, which to someone like Maggie, who floated away on whims, was appealing. Like a helium balloon, she and her mum never knew where Maggie might float off to. Sometimes it felt good when Peter's stark realities and predictable ways seemed to ground her. Didn't it? Maggie was warming to all the quiet things Peter contributed to her life and wanted him to know how much she appreciated him with the gift of a new shirt.

At the library, Maggie situated herself at her favorite study hall table with a pile of books knowing Peter would be rolling his cart by sooner or later.

Hidden in the shadows behind one of the book stacks, Peter had gotten lost in time reading the *Outlander* and didn't realize he'd read nearly two chapters before he cranked up his cart and hit the road again. He drifted on over to Maggie's usual place where he found her smile waiting for him.

"Here, for you! It's a new shirt."

With a bit of hesitancy, she handed the gift to Peter. He looked utterly perplexed at the sight of the carefully wrapped gift.

"Shirt? But I have one."

Peter looked down at his shirt. Yep, it was still there and buttoned all the way up.

"All famous writers have at least two, don't you know? Sure they do. One to wear and one to wash when they're wearing the other one. When you're famous, you'll have a closet full of shirts."

Peter stood there pondering yet another of Maggie's altered-realities.

"But who will iron them?" is all he could come up with.

"I haven't figured that out. Give me time—somehow I'll get around it."

Maggie tweaked his cheek as she didn't want him to walk around the library with lipstick on his face. Peter opened the package and smiled big at the sight of his new bargain shirt.

8

MARY WAS ALWAYS concerned that her Mags would get lost somewhere in her daydreams and simply never show up for work, and therefore no paycheck would show up even as the bills were guaranteed to appear, no matter what. Maggie had lost too many jobs by then for Mary not to know the pattern. And so now that the war was over she figured she'd probably need money for whatever lay ahead for them. Mary determined that finding a house-cleaning job would be in order. She'd kept the addresses of the ladies she'd worked for prior to the war and went through them, looking for the one that might be her best bet for housework. Maybe only a day or two here and there. Just something to keep she and Mags going. She took the few coins she'd squirreled away for a rainy day and bought a bucket and some new brushes. She was going to pay Louisa Harold a call.

But how to get there? It had been before the war started when she'd last been to the Harold's. The tube always seemed loud and threatening, what with all the people bustling and jumping in front of her to be first to get to the exit. She never used it unless Maggie was along. But if she could survive the war, she reasoned, she could take a solo trip on the tube to the other side of London.

Mary planned to keep her little enterprise a secret concerned Maggie would be disapproving of her going back to work. On the following day, she prepared breakfast as usual for Maggie. She knew her daughter would wonder where she was going, what with her old cleaning dress pulled out and ironed up. Mary had to come up with something.

Maggie came in to breakfast early despite having been out late that night with Ann. There, sitting next to the table, sat Mary's bucket, filled with new brushes. With her foot, Mary slowly pushed them under the table and out of sight. Maggie was still half asleep and didn't notice.

"You going out this early, Mum?"

"Best to get to the market early before things are picked over," Mary replied.

"Oh," was all Maggie could get out as she was still only half awake.

Maggie picked up her toast and cup of tea and headed back to bed where she'd catch up on the latest movie star gossip in *Modern Screen* magazine. She bought a copy every week without fail.

As soon as she heard Maggie's old bed springs welcome her back, Mary slipped out the door.

But what if she got lost? She'd thought about that, and thus had filled her coin purse with enough to take several tube trips, one of which would surely land her on Louisa's street and still have enough to get herself close enough to home, whereby she could walk the rest. Isn't that how the tube worked anyway?

Mary could read, at least the signs on the train that showed where the stops were. It had taken her nearly an hour, but she recognized the names of the stops sufficient enough to figure she was headed in the right direction, and then there it was. Like a light flipped on, she first saw Hamstead Tube Station, and then Finchley Road Tube. That was near to where Mrs. Harold lived in Maresfield Gardens, that leafy neighborhood where many well-off people lived in their fine brick homes.

From the tube station, Mary headed down the street, but soon felt herself being pulled in the other direction. She turned and headed that way and soon enough came upon the Harold's big house. She wondered if Louisa would even remember her. But then again, how could she not? She walked up the side of the house to the service door and rang. As she waited, she looked around at all the lovely trees. Had they grown that much since she was here before? Or had she simply never noticed?

Back then, she arrived before the sun came up and left late. But what if Mrs. Harold had moved and the people living there now wouldn't have a clue as to who she was or that she'd worked for Louisa years before? Alas, the door opened, and there stood Louisa Harold in her house dress. She'd hardly changed.

"Why, Mary! It's you!"

She looked down and saw Mary's bucket of brushes sitting next to her worn shoes.

"It is, Ma'am. I came wondering if you needed any help today?"

"Mary, come in. It's been years since I saw you last."

"Before the war, I imagine," Mary replied.

"It was, and I was just wondering who would drop by and have tea with me today, and blessings, here you are!"

Mary smiled. Their friendship had resumed.

"Thank you, Ma'am, and I would love a spot of tea."

"Why are you addressing me as 'Ma'am'? You don't like me after all these years?"

"Of course, I do, Louisa. But it's been ever so long since we last saw each other," Mary said.

"And who was always changing her telephone number during the war?"

"Didn't change it," Mary said. "Had the service cut more than a few times."

"Well, come in. We have so much to catch up on and now we won't need a telephone."

Louisa ushered Mary in. She knew where the breakfast room was as that was where Louisa had her afternoon tea. She gazed about the lovely room, thinking nothing had changed from before the war, unlike almost everywhere else in London. Louisa motioned for Mary to take a seat.

"We'll catch up while the tea steeps. How'd you get here?" Louisa asked.

"The tube, and then I walked. Couldn't remember which way to turn at first, so I just followed my instincts."

"You are so brave taking the tube," Louisa remarked. "I did it during the war, once or twice, as Harold said if I drove his Mercedes, they'd surely stone me for being a German sympathizer. But isn't the Queen driven in a Daimler-Benz?"

"Oh, I reckon not. But I also reckon she's never been seen on the tube either!"

They laughed. Louisa was delighted to see her old friend.

9

As Peter was about to head down for breakfast, he paused as usual before the mirror hanging near his door. But this time, he flipped his part over to the other side. He momentarily studied what he saw before flipping it back again. Then, he adjusted the stiff collar on his new shirt.

"Don't think I look like Tyrone Power," he said to the man looking back from the mirror. Usually they glanced at each other rather suspiciously and only a thought or two were exchanged. But this time, out of the corner of his eye, Peter caught a wink. Didn't he? All the same, he didn't feel much like Tyrone Power that morning.

Downstairs, Mrs. Chapman had his toast ready as always.

"Good morning, Mrs. Chapman. Wanted you to be the first to know."

"Know what, dear?" she asked.

"She gave me a shirt. A shirt!"

Mrs. Chapman chuckled as she buttered his toast.

"Now, who would possibly do that to a nice boy like you?"

"I think I'm in love, and if it stays this way, I may ask her to marry me. Think that's too fast?"

But then what about Alice? Mrs. Chapman wondered. She suddenly became serious and took the seat next to Peter's.

"Well, let's see. How long have you known her?"

"More than two whole months!"

Mrs. Chapman held up two fingers to make sure she got her counting right.

"One… two… Well…." she emphasized. "I'm thinking that's not as long as you might think."

"No, you're right. But actually, it's been two months, two days…" he glanced at his watch, "and six hours."

The numbers were falling in Peter's favor. At least in his vision of things.

"There are lots of very nice girls out there. You have to keep that in mind, and one could be right under your nose. I mean, you don't want to be in a hurry, do you?"

"She gave me a shirt, and it was on sale, too."

"On sale? That's important. Shows she's not foolish with her money. Alice is careful with her money, too. I think she saves most of what she makes."

But Peter was in dreamland, and so what could matter when you're rolling along in the heather? Yes, he was sure he could smell Maggie's hair, even in his daydreams.

"A shirt! For me!"

Peter gulped his tea, grabbed his toast, and headed off to the library wearing his stiff new shirt. Or perhaps it was wearing him.

"Yes, Alice would make a fine wife," Mrs. Chapman said but it was only to herself.

* * *

It was a glorious sunny day when Maggie dragged Peter to Hyde Park. Sundays always had lots of people on the green eating sandwiches as they watched children chasing dogs chasing balls.

First task was to look about for just the right location. Peter said any place was fine; it was a large green. But Maggie said it had to be perfect, and so they spent the next half-hour looking for that 'perfect' place on acres of lawn every inch of which looked strangely the same to Peter.

Finally, with just the perfect place determined, Maggie pulled out the lunch from the basket Peter had been lugging. She'd brought a nice spread for them that Mary had put together. There were finger sandwiches of egg salad, cake, and thankfully, no sauerkraut.

Peter's head rested on her lap as she finger-fed him like a child. He devoured every morsel of it. That is until Maggie filled him in on their plans.

"We'll have to move from London, you know," Maggie announced out of the blue.

Peter nearly choked on the sandwich he was chomping.

"What?" Peter asked. "But I love living at Mrs. Chapman's, and Alice is always so nice to me."

"Alice? Wait, you're right, Petey!" she said and finished Peter's sandwich herself as she rattled off her thoughts as though she was going down a list. She was. Yes, Maggie had it all figured out and then some. That was the portion that concerned Peter the most.

"How will we be able to go to all the posh parties," Maggie wondered, "if we live outside of London? Of course, we'll need a car after we move into the new flat."

"Car?" Peter sat up to hear more. "I don't know how to drive."

"No, of course not. That's what drivers are for."

"Where in London?" he asked, assuming Maggie had determined this as well. She had.

"Well, I'm thinking Chelsea, where all the famous artists live."

"Chelsea? I've never been there," Peter replied.

"You've never been anywhere. It's along the river, no more than twenty odd minutes on the tube from the library."

"What kind of car? You figured that out?"

Of course she had.

"A flashy sporty convertible. Sure. But living in London won't be good for your writing. Too much noise. Might be bad for your concentration, you know." But Peter wasn't sure he knew any such thing and perked up to hear more. "We should have a place near the sea where it's quiet. We can go during the week and return to London on the weekends for parties."

"I've only been to the sea once."

"The clean air will be good for us," she said. "Maybe Torquay, no, I hear Bournemouth is where the smart set go."

"But I'm not one of them."

"You'll get there," Maggie was delighted to inform Peter. "Just keep wearing your new shirt. Townhouse in London, a place near the sea, and a sporty car. Did I leave something out?"

"Just like a movie star," Peter said and let his head fall back on Maggie's lap, where her kisses to his forehead drifted to his lips.

Still, Peter needed something to relieve the shock of having to move, and then learning to drive the car he did not yet possess. What if it wasn't automatic? What color sports car? Not too flashy, he hoped. *Isn't red kind of flashy,* he wondered?

Peter was left wondering about all this. In fact, he was already feeling seasick hearing all those waves crashing against the windows at the beach house Maggie had moved them into between sandwiches. No wonder he couldn't finish the last one. It suddenly seemed soggy, and even tasted a bit like sardines.

By the time Peter had returned to Mrs. Chapman's, she and Alice were just finishing supper. Peter walked in, feeling a bit seasick and car sick from swerving along the road while learning to drive the car he yet had. He was wondering what it would feel like walking around with beach sand in his shoes? Surely it would be bad for the new car's carpeting. And what might his toes have to say about it? Because isn't glass made of melted sand?

"Peter, are you hungry?" Alice asked.

"No, Maggie fed me all day, and not just food."

"Is Maggie your girlfriend?" she asked.

"I guess," is all Peter could get out as he was still stuck wondering why anyone would have a convertible in London, where there are scant few garages and it rains most days.

"Wait, Peter. It's finished. The typing, only two errors. But only tiny ones."

"Thanks, Alice. As long as they're only tiny ones. I stayed awake last night wondering how many errors I'd made. Couldn't think of one, but figured they were probably hiding."

"Would you like me to give your novel to Fred?"

"Yes," Peter replied. "But I guess I should read it one last time first, then I can post it to him. Yes?"

Alice handed the manuscript to Peter along with a smile that fell off a moment later. She had wanted to be the one that brought Peter's work to Fred's attention.

Upstairs Peter washed the sand out of his new shirt so it would be dry for the next day. His daydreams of being at the beach that day had made him feel a bit gritty. *Is the salty sea air bad for the paint on an expensive sports car?* Peter kept wondering, and also if his headache would soon go away.

Down in the kitchen, Mrs. Chapman and Alice were doing the wash-up after supper.

"Why do you think Peter looked so glum?" Mrs. Chapman asked.

"Writers are like that, Mum. When they've finished a big project, it seems they always need a big rest."

"Oh. I hope that's all."

But it wasn't.

10

T HE FOLLOWING WEEK, Maggie was scheduled to work late,
which worked out well as Bulldog Livingston was typically off
the floor doing her paperwork in the afternoons.

"Thank you, Madam. Come back next week for a preview of our
new perfume."

No sooner had the customer walked off than Maggie swept over to
Ann's end of the counter.

"Clock me out at closing. I've got to leave to meet Petey at the library."

"I've clocked you out all week. I could get fired for doing that. I will
get fired for doing that!" Ann screeched.

"What have you lost?" Maggie asked.

"A bloody paycheck!" Ann replied.

Maggie kissed Ann on the cheek and dashed off into the rainy evening.

She was late getting to the library, where she found Peter waiting
outside under his tattered umbrella. The rain was coming down hard.

"Why so dreary?"

"I guess I don't feel like one of your posh people tonight."

"Where is it?" Maggie asked.

Peter handed her the large envelope he'd been protecting under his
raincoat. Inside was his novel manuscript nicely typed by Alice. She
kissed him on the cheek and then glanced at the address on the envelope.

"Fred Morton Agency," she said. "He any good, this Fred Morton
bloke?"

"Of course, he's good or why would Alice work for him?"

"Right. Who is this Alice you go on about?" Maggie didn't wait for a reply. "I'll run for postage in the morning on the way to work and off it goes!"

"Guard it with your life," Peter admonished.

Maggie tucked the manuscript into her coat and put her arm through Peter's. They walked off for a quiet dinner.

* * *

Mary tended to stay up late to make sure Maggie was back safe and sound. Then, she'd tuck her daughter into bed as though she was still a child. But Mary had fallen asleep on the sofa and didn't see Maggie until the next morning at breakfast. She'd made it before her daughter had come into the kitchen.

"Be home late again?" Mary asked, for some reason. If Maggie never knew if she was coming or going what difference would a clock make. After all, there's no such thing as being late if one makes it a point to never be on time.

"Don't know. It's raining," Maggie replied.

"I'll put a plate back for you."

"Yeah, Mum. Put a plate back."

She kissed Mary on the cheek and sat down to eat. Mary put her toast in front of her and Maggie started to put jam on, but realized she'd forgotten the butter first. She tossed the toast back on her plate.

"Everything okay, dear?"

"Yes, Mum. Everything's fine. Just a lot on my mind."

Maggie grabbed one of the umbrellas waiting in the corner of the kitchen and started to head out.

"You left something," Mary said.

Maggie looked over her outfit; both shoes were on, hat on.

"What?"

Mary pointed to the large envelope with Peter's manuscript still on the table.

"Thanks, Mum!"

Maggie grabbed it and dashed out the door.

"Always running for something…" Mary said to herself and sat down to eat Maggie's toast.

The tube was particularly busy, as it always is on gray days when no one chanced walking to work in a drizzle.

Aboard, she moved through the crowd until she found a couple of seats. She took a deep breath and placed her purse, umbrella, overcoat over Peter's manuscript on the seat next to her.

It wasn't long before a handsome man noticed Maggie. Well, they always noticed her. He smiled, and then smiled again, but she ignored him until he worked his way over.

"Is it always this bad?" he asked, showing his nicely polished wisdom teeth at the end of his smile.

"Huh? What?" Maggie asked and pulled out her compact and reapplied her lipstick.

"The tube," he said. "At this time of day, I mean. I'm new to London. I'm David. Accountant in the City."

Maggie had other things on her mind, and it wasn't some guy looking for a weekend date.

She looked up to David and winked.

"David, I'm Maggie. Unemployed whore looking for work. Wanna be my friend?"

The smile on David's handsome face slid off like he'd just walked into a glass door. The other passengers stared at Maggie. David couldn't ease himself away fast enough. Maggie's words followed.

"Hey, big boy. Weren't you the one who gave me the clap that time? Or was it that the other David, a big accountant in the City. There's so many Davids out there and only one of me, hey?"

The passengers became glued to the drama. Maggie rolled her eyes at them and pulled out her lipstick again. It was always her therapy, and anyway, it was raining, and everyone was out of sorts.

The train reached her stop and it appeared as though everyone was as eager to get off at the same station. Dreading the rain up on the street, Maggie grabbed her purse, umbrella, and overcoat and started for the gate along with a herd of passengers.

Outside, from the rain, Maggie held her raincoat over her head and then suddenly realized she was not in possession of her big brown envelope.

Maggie went yelling back down the steps to the train platform.

"Stop!" she screeched. "Stop! The tracks are broken, or bent, or going the wrong way!"

Well, things happen! They sure enough do and that can be when the misery kicks in!

It had been a miserable morning, and the worst was to come; she was late for work.

"What happened?" Ann asked. "You look like a wet dog."

"Was on the tube. Some bloke tried to pick me up, and the rain…"

"Livingston just made her rounds," Ann interrupted. "I told her you were in the loo. If she sees your hair, she'll wonder if your head was in the toilet."

"Can someone drown herself in a toilet? I'm off to find out."

Maggie started to walk off, but Ann caught her wet sleeve and tugged her back.

"Here, tie your hair back with this scarf until it dries," Ann directed and pulled off the one around her neck. "Oh, and you've made six sales. I showed your book to Livingston, but she just walked away like she didn't believe it."

"She's probably noticed that your writing looks a lot like mine," Maggie said. "Even if she never sees me around."

Ann dabbed Maggie's tears.

"Maggie, what's wrong?" she asked. "We've all had rainy-day Mondays."

"Not like this one. It's much worse! I think I'm drowning."

"You think?"

Maggie shook her head. The thorny words were stuck deep in her throat.

She was quiet that day; unusually quiet particularly as her prattling on with Ann always seemed to make the day go by faster. Before long, Bulldog Livingston had made her last round, and Maggie felt safe enough to go get dolled up. She knew that something was brewing with Peter, and she was anxious about what it was. But then again, she had something truly awful to confess and didn't know how she would handle it. She'd been thinking about it all gray-long day, yet she still hadn't come up with the right story she'd tell.

"Date with Peter tonight?" Ann asked.

"I think he's going to…"

Maggie couldn't quite get the words out. Strangely, she felt as though she was still dripping wet from that morning. Well, she was, in a way. Maybe a bit like having your head held under the water until, and if, you can yell "uncle." Sometimes, just that one word can do you in if you can't seem to get it out.

"Is Peter going to ask you to? What? To marry him? Is he?"

At first, Maggie couldn't say the word. She reached for a bottle of fragrance and spritzed herself.

"Congrats!" Ann said. "I'll have one, too."

She grabbed the bottle of fragrance and sprayed herself.

"Hey, it's still alcohol," Ann said. "It'll be champagne at the wedding, hey?"

"Annie, I'm in trouble," Maggie whispered.

"Trouble?" The only thing you could be in trouble for is if you're pregnant and from another boyfriend."

"No. There's no other boyfriend."

Maggie was obviously exasperated.

"Ah… Please kill me!"

"Funny, I've been thinking of it for weeks now!" Ann replied.

"Stand in line!" Maggie replied.

Maggie pasted on a smile of sorts, and with her chin up, went off to face Peter with the bad news.

11

I**T WAS A** special bistro that Peter took them to. It only confirmed to Maggie what was coming as he never splashed out for fancy food at fancy places. But this place held special meaning for them.

Peter was in a cheery mood and couldn't seem to sit still. Maggie wasn't, and swayed in her seat like she wanted to be some other place and get there quick.

"This is the first place we had dinner together, not including the…" Maggie finished his sentence.

"The fish and chips stand where you got sick?"

"I'm wearing my new shirt," he announced.

"It's not new anymore," she demurred.

All Maggie could think was that she could have saved herself from this moment if Ann had only let her drown herself in the toilet that morning.

"What's wrong?" Peter asked.

"I have something to tell you. You're not going to be happy when you hear this. In fact, you're going to hate me," she said without looking Peter in the eyes.

But Peter didn't take her seriously as Maggie's humor was always a bit dark.

"But wait. I have something special to ask you first."

Maggie looked away as her eyes filled with tears. Peter smiled, figuring she knew what he was about to ask. *Clearly, she was beside herself with joy*, he thought. But the real drama was about to unfold.

Peter took her hands into his and leaned over the table.

"Then you know what I'm going to ask you, don't you? You know I love you, Maggie," but Maggie couldn't bear to hear what Peter was about to propose, and cut him off. Her words pounced on the Peter's moment.

"Petey, I have some bad news. It's about your novel…" she blurted before Peter could open his mouth again.

There was a long silence. Then Peter noticed that Maggie couldn't seem to look him in the eyes.

"My novel? What do you mean? What about it?"

Then she hit him with the news. She told him everything that had happened on the tube that morning. Well, almost. Yes, she'd left out one crucial detail. Peter sat stupefied after Maggie lowered the bad news. He started to speak, but the words wouldn't come and yet his mouth couldn't close. The special dinner that Peter had rehearsed in his mind, and then again in his daydreams for weeks, the one where their lives would go on joyously entwined, could not have gone worse.

Just as Maggie rose to leave, the waiter arrived with the menus. But the party was all over and then some. Watching Maggie head to the exit, Peter dabbed his tears hoping no one noticed him suddenly sitting alone with two menus staring back. At least the paper had caught his tears as they fell off his cheeks. There was nothing at hand to catch his broken heart; the pieces lay scattered across the bottom of his misery.

Out on the street again, Maggie decided to walk home rather than take the tube. She needed to cry off the pain caused by Peter's expression when she told him the bad news. She knew it had been a double punch. His tearful eyes had told it all. She would see them in her nightmares in the days and weeks ahead. But things were actually much worse than that. They would be soon be catastrophic for both of them and many others.

* * *

Mary was sitting by the fireplace knitting a bulky sweater when Maggie got in. She'd not told her mum what she was anticipating from Peter that night. In fact, she'd not told her much of anything of late.

Maggie slumped into her bedroom to put her things away and returned to flop down on the sofa and took a deep breath. Mary held her sweater up next to her big smile.

"Look, almost finished!"

"Mum, I'm never gonna wear that. Not in public, anyway."

Mary could see that her daughter's eyes were red and puffy. She went over and sat next to her daughter.

"That's okay," Mary said. "I was really knitting it for myself. It's my favorite color. Look at you. What's wrong? Why are you crying?"

"Mum, Petey asked me to marry him tonight."

"He asked you? Tonight?"

"Yes, Mum. That's what I said."

Mary was eager to hear more and grasped Maggie's hand, but she pulled back and looked off.

"… and I told him 'no,' " she confessed.

Mary was stunned; she'd grown so fond of Peter.

"You did what?"

Maggie became really agitated.

"No, Mum. No! I can't marry Petey now."

"Why? He's a good boy. He's going to be a famous writer come one day," Mary said. "We both know he is."

"No, he isn't." Maggie announced. "No,….. he isn't."

"Whatever do you mean, dear?"

"Mum, I lost Petey's novel. Left it on the tube on my way to post it."

Mary started to choke when she heard this.

"You left it on the tube?" she screeched. "He worked for years on that novel. You lost it? How? How, I said!"

At that moment, Mary started belting Maggie with her bulky sweater still knotted up with her knitting needles.

"You careless, silly girl!" Mary yelled.

"Mum, stop! Stop!" Maggie howled. "I don't know! I don't know anything. How else are we going to make it?"

"What?" Mary demanded. "What do you mean?"

"Never mind, Mum. You wouldn't understand!"

"So, try anyway. I'm your mum."

Maggie's emotions had suddenly jumped to wholesale anger.

"Petey, in the end, he's not really going to marry me!"

"I don't understand," Mary said. "What does that have to do with Peter's novel?"

"You know Petey isn't and so do I, so there! You finally got it out of me! Are you happy? No, you're never happy, Mum! Not with me anyway!"

"Why do you say that?" Mary asked. "Why would he ask you if he wasn't going to? I'm so confused now."

"Why would he, that's why! What can I give him? I can't even read or write and look where that's left us. I can't even get a decent job."

"Oh, dear, there's so much more to it than that," Mary said.

"Yeah, Mum? How would you know? You met Dad, had a kid, and he couldn't get out the door fast enough! And then what? You bought a bucket and some brushes to remember him by."

"But we've gotten by, Mags! How's it different for anyone?"

"Get by, is it? Well, I don't want to have a kid and then wait for the father to take off when something better walks by in a skirt and I end up spending my life scrubbing floors. That's not getting by in my book!"

"Oh, dear, Mags. I never knew you felt this way," Mary replied. "Did I once do something to make you so angry?"

"And then what about you if I got married?" Maggie demanded. "How can I take care of you if a man doesn't want a mum around? Did you ever think of that? Well, I do every day!"

"But Peter likes me, doesn't he?"

"Sure, Mum. Don't they all say it when they want in? But then their tune changes, hey? Just look at Dad. Out the door the day you walked in the door with me."

"Maggie, you don't know the half of it."

"No, Mum?" Maggie said. "Then you tell me how it works even if it didn't for you! Hey, Mum?"

Mary tossed her knitting to the floor and embraced her daughter. Her motherly instincts told her there was a much larger drama brewing and she was ever so right.

Maggie shook her head, wiped a tear, kissed Mary on the cheek and went to her room.

That night, Maggie lay in her bed crying. She tossed and turned, but the pain of what she'd done that day was hardly going to leave her soon. No, she knew she'd done a very bad deed. But it was actually much worse than that because she reached under her pillow and pulled out Peter's manuscript she'd tucked there when she walked in. She had, after all, made it back on the train that day, went to where she had been sitting, and pulled the manuscript out from under the fat woman who unknowingly was nesting on that big brown envelope.

Maggie kissed the manuscript and slid it back under her mattress. This was the beginning of a train ride that would hurl Maggie in all directions, landing her in worlds she'd only glanced at from borrowed books on movie stars. Those distant places she'd always longed to escape to… and take her mum with her. She'd figured she had just come by the very ticket that would convey her to those glittery destinations she'd only seen pictures of in books about movie stars.

12

T HE MORNING AFTER Maggie broke the news and so much more, Peter headed to work like he always did. But that day, he could barely crawl there. No, things were not going well. His proposal for a lifetime of love had been turned down by this confounding creature with the red lips, and, on top of the soul-bludgeoning, he'd been informed that his novel was gone for good. His churning stomach kept reminding him he was closer to the edge of nothing than he'd ever experienced in his well-ordered and ever so predictable life. Now all he seemed to be able to do with ease was cry. He sat on the floor in a dark corner of the library, hidden by his book cart stacked high with books, and let the faucets pour. The tears chased after his runny nose. Why go on if life is so miserable? That was the only voice he heard piercing his thoughts that dark morning. Yeah, and that voice keep asking him if he was really thinking of throwing himself on the train tracks. Things can happen if you will them hard enough and have the courage to take that last step. And then there's no more pain.

But then, in a flash, it was as though a bright light had turned back on. Peter suddenly conjured a notion that he'd gotten it all wrong. Sure, he had! It's not like he really understood Maggie; in fact, he didn't understand her at all—he only gauged her words by reading her expressions and left the rest of it, including her frequent looniness, on the banks of the moment.

Peter jumped up with the notion that perhaps Maggie would be sitting at her favorite library table, thumbing through her books on movie stars just waiting for his smile. Whatever happened the night before, he reasoned, they could always talk it out, as they always did. *Things can happen*, he reminded himself, but one can get past it.

About then he was sure he'd heard Maggie's voice. That laugh he knew so well. He hurried his cart towards the table and slowly pulled a book off the shelf to peek through. But, no, Maggie was not there, nor was there a stack of books about movie stars suggesting she'd been by. It had been some other woman he'd heard laughing and thought was Maggie. The tears trickled down again, but there weren't many left at that point. He wiped his nose and retreated with his cart to another dark corner to tend his wounds. Still, Maggie's laughing voice seemed to follow his every pained thought that day.

* * *

Mary and Maggie had always kept an eye on each other, mostly to keep the other out of scrapes, or perhaps to point the finger for the woes that seemed to always broadside them. When you can't pay the bills, the troubles come like the rains and so do the recriminations. And now there were a good number of scrapes headed their way.

Mary may have been successful at slipping away to Louisa's without Maggie noticing, but not so with the neighbors. The women were chatting outside their doors when Mary departed for the day.

"You headed off to market again today?" Primrose asked.

"Yes. Always forget what I went for the day before, don't I?" Mary said. But her bucket of brushes hummed a different tune.

"Why the bucket?" Dora asked.

"Why the brushes? Primrose asked.

"Makes me look official, don't you think?" Mary asked.

Primrose and Dora nodded and smiled as Mary headed off.

"Official?" Dora asked.

"What's that mean?" Primrose asked.

"You think she's running for Parliament?" Dora asked.

"You never know with Mary. But I'll put a vote in for her no matter!"

* * *

Well, life goes on, Maggie thought as she boarded the tube for work. That was her tonic to get through the tangles. She even showed up on time at Selfridge's. Business was brisk that morning, with lots of women looking for the new shade of lipstick or some tinted powder.

"Will this be on your account, Madam?" Ann asked.

"Yes, please," the customer replied.

Once Ann had finished wrapping the purchase and handed it to the customer Maggie was already pulling out her bag.

"I'm headed for lunch," Maggie whispered over to Ann. "Need to run an errand if Bulldog happens by with her whip.

"If you don't get back on time, I'm not clocking you out tonight!" Ann announced.

"Sure, you will!" Maggie replied and tweaked Ann's cheek as had become their ritual. "I'll be right back after lunch. Say four or five."

Ann failed to see the humor as she was left with unpacking the new merchandise.

It was a sunny day, and lots of people were out and about on High Street. Maggie sighted the notary shop someone had told her about and dashed in. The notary greeted her from behind the counter, which was stacked with official looking papers and forms she was sorting.

"How may we help?" the woman asked.

"Do you type?" Maggie asked.

"Why, yes. We have a typing service."

Maggie pulled out the large envelope with Peter's manuscript and pulled the papers out and handed the first page to the notary.

"Type something that looks like this. I'll tell you what to change."

"You just need the title page retyped?" the notary asked.

"Yeah. A new one."

"Yes, I can do that for you now," the notary replied and went over to her typewriter.

"What should I type?"

"I'm changing the title. Ah, the novel is now *My Last Lives*, by, what's a fancy writer's name? Oh, how about Olivia Holiday? How's that sound?"

"Yes, Ma'am."

The notary typed the new title page and in moments handed it to Maggie.

"This look right?" she asked.

"How should I know? Does it read as I asked?"

"You can't read?" the perplexed notary asked.

"Of course, I can read. How could I write a novel if I can't read? I just don't have my reading glasses.

"Well, it's just as you dictated, Miss Holiday," she said.

"That sounds good. Especially the Miss Holiday part!" Maggie replied. "How much?"

Maggie handed her a coin and grabbed the new page to her new novel and left to work on her new life. Yep, there was a train, a special train that somewhere in her daydreams had been waiting for Maggie to board. It was about to depart for a journey of a lifetime. It sure as hell was! The problem was that Maggie hadn't purchased a ticket. But then, Maggie seldom got bogged down in the details of life. Nope, she tended to just grab on for dear life! Wherever she was headed, it had to be better than where she took off from. Well, Joan Crawford would have understood! She, too, was a survivalist.

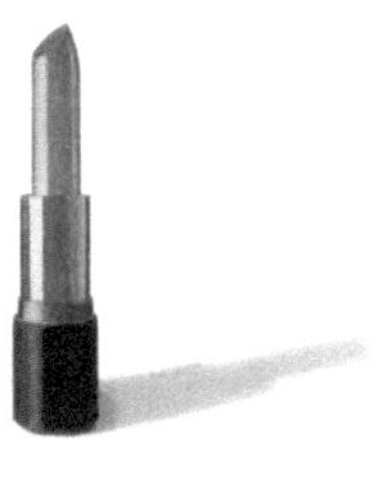

13

F or **Peter, the** week could not have been darker. He'd lost his girlfriend along with his manuscript, and so felt like a sinking ship slowly taking on water. *When was the actual moment*, he wondered, *when it all came apart?* Things happen, don't they? But if you don't know exactly where and when, how do you come to terms with the why of it all? Why had Maggie jumped ship just as he was about to propose?

Peter came downstairs at Mrs. Chapman's for breakfast that Friday, already wondering what he would do over the weekend, that is if it ever came around for him. He wasn't going to be writing a new novel—that much he knew.

"Peter, you've been awfully quiet the last few days," Alice noted.

"He's waiting to hear back from Fred about his manuscript," Mrs. Chapman said and placed Peter's toast in front of him.

Peter could hardly hold back the tears as the week before, he'd tossed away all the handwritten pages Alice had returned to him once she'd typed them.

"Oh my god, Peter. What is it?" Mrs. Chapman asked.

At that, Peter started to wail.

"Maggie, she lost my novel last week. Left it on the tube."

"So, it was never posted to the agent?" Alice asked.

"No. It's gone forever."

"And I knew I should have taken it in myself!" Alice said.

"Your novel is gone? Lost?" Mrs. Chapman asked, trying to make out what had happened through Peter's sobs.

But things happen.

Seeing Peter in such distress brought tears to Alice.

"No, Peter, it's not gone, just lost for now." Alice said quietly, almost to herself.

"What do you mean?" Mrs. Chapman asked.

"I typed it on carbon paper. All the offices do that now. I have a copy, just need to retype it on regular paper."

Peter wiped his tears and jumped up to kiss Alice.

"Oh, thank you, Alice! I love you!"

Mrs. Chapman smiled at Alice. She was always proud of her daughter.

"How long will it take, dear?"

"A month or so. I'll work on it a bit every night. But Peter must do my wash-ups while I work on his typing," Alice said.

"Good! I'll have someone to talk to when I'm burning holes ironing your blouses."

Life had suddenly cranked up again, and Peter rolled up his sleeves, ready for action.

"Where's the dishpan?"

Yep, things can sure happen and sometimes right out of the blue.

* * *

Mary showed up early that Wednesday. Louisa had given her the key to let herself in, but she'd already been up baking scones. They were cooling on the table next to a pot of red currant jam when Mary came in.

"Good morning, Louisa. I wasn't going to come today, you know, the rain, but I could smell those scones all the way from Pilimco."

"I knew you'd not be able to stay away—that's why I kept them in the oven until just before you walked up. Sit down, the kettle is on."

Mary went over to the silver pantry and pulled out a piece along with a rag and the silver polish.

"I've got to do something while we talk, or I won't have earned my coin for the day," Mary said.

"Mary, at our age? Why in the world would we care if the floors need a sweep or the silver a polish? I haven't used those silver pieces in years. Sit down, dear. After we eat these scones, I'll make us sandwiches and then we'll pull out the gin if we get bored."

"You really shouldn't work me so hard, Louisa. I may come to file a complaint at the labor board one day!"

"Is that right! For that, you get two gin and tonics. One to take home with you on the tube," Louisa replied. "Think of it as a bribe so you don't turn me in!"

It didn't take these women long to finish off the scones. By that time, they'd worked so hard, worked their mouths, that is, that they were hungry again.

"I'm going to make some special sandwiches." Louisa announced.

"What kind today?" Mary asked.

"Smoked salmon from Scotland on slices of cucumber."

"But Louisa, that's what I eat every day."

"Me, too!" Louisa said. "You know Harold was a very generous man."

"Yes, he was," Mary confirmed.

"I loved him till the day he died, and then I went off shopping and haven't really come home since! You know, one has to deal with grief the best one can."

"And Harold was always nice to me, too!" Mary added.

"Yes, he truly was a good man." Louisa replied. "Good to me, good to the neighbor woman I came to find out, and, I reckon, good to every-thing that passed along wearing a skirt."

Mary giggled as Louisa refilled her glass.

The memories were always spicy around Louisa's breakfast table and there were yet more to come. Much more!

14

MAGGIE WAS LATE to work as always, and even when she was there, her spirit seldom was. Lest she run into Livingston making her rounds, she headed to the cosmetics counter like a tornado.

"Need a really smart outfit. Is it nicking if you borrow one but bring it back?" she asked Ann.

"Talk to Sylvia up on fancy dress. She'll find you something."

Maggie dashed for the backstairs as she stopped taking the escalators in the event Bulldog was on the lookout. Within an hour, Maggie was dressed to the nines and back out on High Street. But first, how do you find a literary agency in London if you can't read addresses? Maggie was already up against a serious conundrum. She decided to stop to think things out. Like Maggie always said, 'I'll get around it.' About then, she spotted a coffee house and went in to sit down as her toes were feeling pinched from those fancy new shoes she'd borrowed.

"A coffee with lots of cream and sugar," Maggie told the waiter. "I haven't eaten today."

The waiter was soon back, and placed a large cup of coffee in front of her, along with a pitcher of cream and a bowl of sugar cubes. She poured cream into her cup. It was too hot, so she sat there still contemplating what would be her next move that day. About then, the woman sitting with her back to Maggie turned around and smiled.

"Any cream left, honey? I never have cream at home because I'm so used to drinking tea from my school days," the woman said. "I'm Phyllis. I was a teacher you know."

At that, Maggie realized her conundrum on finding a literary agency was near to being resolved.

"Really? Teacher, you say? Well, at least they gave you something," Maggie said. "You know, I have an appointment today at a literary agency. But I left home without the address. Can you believe?"

Phyllis was momentarily puzzled; she had no idea what that meant to her.

"Where do you think I can find the address?"

"Try back there at the ladies room," Phyllis said. "There's a telephone book, I'm sure. Go back and see if the proper address is in there."

"Yes, but I forgot my reading glasses. Be a dear and go back and tear out the page of literary agencies while I order you a piece of pie to go with that coffee. Yes?"

"I'll be right back. Cherry will be fine!"

Phyllis headed back to the lady's room as Maggie reached for the woman's cup of coffee and placed it on her table and waved the waiter over.

"You have cherry pie?"

"Yes, Miss."

"How much is a piece?"

He bent over to whisper.

"If you give me your phone number, it's on the house."

"Then I'll have two pieces as my phone number is particularly long!"

The waiter left with a big smile just as Phyllis returned.

"Here, sit and talk to me while we eat our cherry pie. He's bringing it straight away."

Phyllis sat down and handed the torn page from the telephone book to Maggie.

"Surely the office you're looking for is on this page. Which one looks like the right one?"

Maggie looked at the torn paper as if she could read; that is, if she had had her reading glasses.

"Be a dear. Which one of these places look the best to you?"

"Best, you say?"

"You know, which literary agency. One that might have lots of important authors making lots of money."

"You mean you don't recall which one you have an appointment at?"

"How silly of me! So much on my mind these days! But I'm sure it was a really important one." Maggie said. "Which is the fanciest looking agency on the fanciest street in the poshest district? That surely must be the right one for me, don't you think?"

"I have no idea, but I'll circle two or three that look like they're important so you can tell the taxi. That sound about right?"

"Yes, it sure enough does. How's your cherry pie?"

"Delicious!" Phyllis said. "You know, I haven't had cherry pie since the war started!"

"I should take your phone number so we can do this again one day!"

Phyllis smiled and scribbled her phone number on a scrap of paper and handed it to Maggie.

"Got to go!"

Maggie grabbed the phone number and the page from the phone book and got up to leave. There at the door, she ran into the waiter.

"How was the cherry pie, Miss?"

"Great! Here's my phone number."

Maggie handed the waiter Phyllis' phone number and slipped out smiling ear to ear. She was on a roll!

* * *

The sign above the door said it all; "Famous Writers' Agency, Ltd." Maggie thought she was in luck; that is, until she walked in.

Five steps into the office and Maggie was waving away clouds of cigarette smoke just to see across reception. Far off into the gray haze sat a woman bent over her old desk flipping through papers. Her nose was only inches from her task as the smoke was so heavy she could hardly see what she was doing. She didn't appear to see Maggie through the haze. The ashtray piled high with butts suggested she'd been there for some time.

Waving the cigarette smoke out of her face, Maggie approached the woman.

"Yes?" the woman said. She'd barely got the word out when she blew smoke into Maggie's well-made-up face. Betty was her name.

"Here's what: if you blow smoke my way again," Maggie said, "I'll blow your head off so hard it will land on Hitler's lap!"

"What?" Betty screeched. "He's dead! Don't you know anything?"

"Well now, I sure enough know we both speak German."

"So, then how can I help you, Miss?" A very perturbed Betty asked. She put her cigarette out by stubbing it so many times that the tin ashtray vibrated butts over the table.

"Who is the most powerful agent in this place? The one that works with famous writers like it says in the telephone directory?" Maggie asked. "That's the one I want to talk to."

Betty looked Maggie up and down suspiciously and then pointed across the room to an old painting of a handsome young man. It was so nicotine-stained that one could barely make out the image.

"Him?" Maggie queried.

She squinted to see through the brown stain.

"That was Mr. Finchley… fifty years ago."

"So, he's dead?" Maggie asked.

"Not quite," Betty whispered. "He's got no one in there now. Go back and see if his heart is still beating. He'll be glad to show you, I'm sure."

"Show me?" Maggie said. "Show me what?"

At that Betty giggled loud enough to be heard on the street.

"No heart beat and I can leave early today."

"But what if it is?" Maggie quizzed. "His heart still beating, I mean."

"Then you're in luck, if that's what you want to call it."

Betty yelled across reception to Finchley's door.

"Mr. Finchley, a young woman to see you."

"A woman?" Finchley yelled back, suggesting he was indeed alive, or mostly. "To see me?" He said suggesting he had a bit of memory left from days of fore!

A woman? He sounded as though this couldn't possibly be the case. Maggie could only have wondered if all his 'famous authors' were men. Just then, Mr. Finchley stepped out of his office—all five feet tall and five feet wide of him. He could only have moved faster if he'd rolled himself out. Tumbled?

"Come in, my dear. Yes, of course, come right in."

Finchley had a big smile that displayed his brown teeth, or at least the few he had left.

"What a delight," he said, and motioned for Maggie to enter his office.

"I'll bring in your morning tea, Mr. Finchley," Betty announced.

"I'm sure you will, Betty."

But Mr. Finchley only had eyes for Maggie.

"Come in and have a seat. Tell Finch, that's what my friends call me, all about it."

Finchley waddled over to his desk and plopped into his chair. He motioned for Maggie to take the chair across from his desk, which she did after pushing the pile of papers over to the floor. That pile of papers looked to have been there so long they were as brown as Finchley's teeth.

"Now, what brings you here today? Go ahead and tell me about it."

"About what?" Maggie asked. She wished he'd stop smiling as his mouth strangely reminded her of Betty's ashtray.

"I wrote a novel, well, anyway, and I want to have it published. Yes, there it is."

Well, at least part of that was truthful. Yep, she wanted to be a novelist because that was near to being a movie star, at least somewhere in Maggie's celluloid rendered daydreams.

A moment later, Betty showed with two cups of tea. She placed one in front of Maggie and the other Finch. Maggie cringed. The cup, which hadn't been washed since the Norman invasion, was also the color of Finch's teeth. Maggie was starting to see a pattern. A very disconcerting one at that!

"Thank you, Betty. Now shut the door," Finchley directed, and went back to bombarding Maggie with smiles

Maggie caught a glimpse of Betty looking at her as though she'd soon be finding out what she'd walked herself into.

Maggie pulled out the manuscript and reached over the table, where she placed it in front of the agent to the famous authors. Without glancing at the manuscript, Finch smiled with obvious delight and attempted to sip his tea.

"Ouch! Betty, I told you not so hot!" he screeched through the door. "I swear, that woman out there doesn't speak English. I can't read very well," he said to Maggie, and that was surely something she could relate to. "Why don't you come around my desk and sit here in front of me, so we can see how I can help you."

What did he just say? Maggie wondered. *Perch on his desk in front of him, is it?*

Finchley patted the desk directly in front of him, where he wished for Maggie to situate herself for him to see… how he could help her. Maggie smiled, and that truly delighted Finch. His smile suggested, that the way things were progressing, they were near to being on the same page. But Maggie had other ideas. She sure did. She walked around his desk, her red lips smiling ear to ear, picked up his cup of too hot tea, and slowly, ever so slowly, poured it over Finchley's crotch.

He howled! But it wasn't in a language Maggie understood. Maybe German?

"My willy! You scalded my willy, you damned bitch."

Maggie took exception to Mr. Finchley's encapsulation of their moment. She picked up her manuscript, along with her own cup of tea,which she proceeded to pour over his bald pate and headed to the door. It hardly mattered what Finchley thought of her writing; it seemed unlikely he was going to make her a famous novelist.

Hearing the commotion from reception, Betty choked laughing as she lit up again.

"Sounds like the old man doesn't speak German either. Hey?"

Well, the day wasn't over, and Maggie still had the name of an agency or two she might wish to visit.

* * *

It was the second on the list of literary agencies Phyllis had circled. She stood outside for a few moments before deciding to enter. Well, the Brandon Literary Agency was a fancy-looking place because it was very successful and wanted everyone to know. So, isn't that how things worked for the rich and famous?

Maggie slipped into the agency almost as though she didn't want anyone to notice her. Sandra, sitting at reception, did notice, and looked her up and down as if she was just as out of place as Maggie felt.

"Golly! Posh as hell," Maggie said, mostly to herself.

Sandra kept eyeing her. She was the agency's gatekeeper, assigned the task of keeping writers without appointments from dropping by to drop their manuscripts on her lap.

"This is a very successful agency," Sandra remarked disdainfully, as if Maggie was an uninvited guest at the wrong private members' club. Still, that sounded good enough to Maggie, who had plans—big plans. Yes, she planned to start at the top and work her way up from there. And she aimed to do it fast!

"Why are you here again? Sandra asked. "I know you don't have an appointment, do you?"

"I sure as hell do! Now!" Maggie said and moved her hand over the fine upholstery of the chairs situated across from Sandra's desk, as big as any banker's in the City.

"I'm Olivia Holiday."

Sandra was skeptical that Maggie was anybody. The big dress-up and fancy, movie star-like name failed to convince her otherwise.

"Right. We all are, aren't we? At least somewhere in time."

"Pardon…?"

Maggie looked about the posh office as Sandra looked at Maggie's shoes. Well, they did match her suit even if they weren't hers. Maggie dropped the manuscript, Peter's manuscript, on Sandra's desk. Yes, she meant business and there was proof of it. Well, sort of.

But Sandra simply looked at it like it was yesterday's uneaten baloney sandwich and then proceeded to flip through her appointment book but still not looking at the pages she was flipping. What? Nope, she was looking right at Maggie to see how long it would be before she got the message.

"Appointment? Don't seem to see you. Don't see you at all, do I?" Sandra remarked and kept flipping pages. Certainly Maggie felt a bit invisible at that moment. But then it clicked.

"Oh, I get it."

Maggie pulled out a whole pound and tossed it onto Sandra's appointment book to help her see better. Instantly Sandra's vision improved.

"He'll know who I am," Maggie announced and wondered if that would bring an invitation to be seated on the fancy upholstery that surely no one had ever sat on. It didn't.

"Really? Who will?" Sandra asked.

Maggie smiled and wondered how many birds she could get with one stone?

"The best-looking agent you have! Why not?" she announced, and pulled out her tube of lipstick to demonstrate she was armed for the takedown.

Sandra scooped up Maggie's pound.

"Oh, yes, of course. Looks like you could be with Brandon. Hey?"

"Could be? Is he the best looking one?" Maggie asked.

"Well, in that case…"

At that, Sandra went back to flipping the pages of her appointments book. And then, after a long pause, she flipped them back again and somewhere in the middle she seemed to stall. To help make the trip shorter, Maggie pulled out another pound. Only this time she didn't toss it on the appointments book. No, she waved it about like a dainty hanky waiting to see what she'd get in return.

"Surely it must be Brandon, then! He's decidedly the best-looking agent here!" Sandra said.

With that, Maggie flipped the pound onto Sandra's appointments book and she quickly grabbed it.

"So, how many agents do you have?" Maggie asked. "Maybe I should look have a look."

"Just one. Brandon. Take him or leave him?"

Thinking of her experience with "Finch", she asked for reinforcements.

"What would you do?" Maggie asked.

"I definitely take him!" Sandra replied.

"Taken. I'm out of money anyway!" Maggie announced.

With that, Sandra picked up the manuscript, about like she'd pulled it out of the garbage, and headed towards Brandon's office door.

Maggie stood there looking puzzled.

"Coming?" Sandra beckoned.

Maggie followed her into an even posher office. The table behind Brandon's desk was strewn with photographs of all the famous writers he knew, or at least that's what Maggie reasoned. To her, they only looked like the images of politicians she'd seen in newspapers. Not one of them looked like a famous, or even once-famous movie star. Nor was one near as pretty as Tyrone Power.

"Your one o'clock is here," she announced to Brandon, a handsome man pouring over piles of papers and looking as though he was near to drowning in oozing paper pulp.

"Sure looks talented to me," Sandra said. "Don't you, Miss? Here's her manuscript to prove it."

Sandra again gave Maggie the once over.

"She's turned down six agents just this morning. Haven't you, Miss… 'Holiday'? I get that right?"

"I have a one o'clock?" he asked. "It's not in my book," Brandon said looking puzzled.

"Oh, I forgot to update your book," Sandra said, and winked at

Maggie. She knew Brandon was likely to take an appointment with a beautiful woman.

"I'm Olivia Holiday, but my friends call me Maggie."

Brandon was easily taking by Maggie's stunning appearance. Sandra reached across his desk and placed the manuscript in front of Brandon along with a wink left.

"Have a seat, Miss… Holiday."

Brandon gestured to the fancy chair across from his desk.

She wondered if it had once been a throne. Well, important people like to sit high, don't they? As Maggie sat fidgeting, Brandon thumbed through the pages that had just been dropped in front of him. Seemed like nearly every page or so he turned, he glanced up at this Miss Holiday who'd just parachuted into his day.

"Interesting," he said.

"Is that good?" Maggie said before thinking she best come up with something better, but couldn't.

"Most writers who come to me, I'm talking about ones who actually have appointments, drop by with pages that are nearly unreadable. Your style is crisp and yet lyrical even from the first page."

And that all sounded a bit good to Maggie. She kept repeating his words in her head to make sure she got it right.

"Well, that's good. Must be!" Surely had to have been something Joan Crawford would have said to Louis B Meyer at MGM.

"Leave your manuscript with me, and we'll get back to you soon."

"Get back to me?" Maggie asked anxiously. What was that likely to actually mean? Like, what if he went and left it on the tube?

"Soon," Brandon repeated and rose to offer his hand to shake.

Maggie extended her hand, and having no idea what to do next, slowly backed out of his office.

Brandon could only have wondered why she was walking backwards. But then again, most people tended to look at Maggie as though she was a bit strange, so she didn't think anything of it when Brandon smiled when she backed into the wall.

15

After spending most of the morning scouting agents' offices, Maggie headed back to her job. She was hopeful that Bulldog would be at lunch and not notice her late arrival. Of course, Ann had clocked her in so she wouldn't miss any pay.

It had been a long and exciting morning what with a borrowed outfit, a borrowed manuscript, and a trip to a literary agent's office, where the receptionist appeared to think she was borrowing trouble. Well, wasn't she? Yep, even the cherry pie that morning had been borrowed along with the telephone number that paid for it.

Maggie quickly got to work, which meant she spent the time until closing filling Ann in on her escapades that morning. By the time they'd had a tea break or two, it was already time to go home.

By the time Maggie got back to the flat that evening, she wasn't in the mood to chat much. All the way home on the tube, she'd wondered if her escapades at the Brandon Literary Agency would get her packed off to Australia where they send book nickers. *All book nickers*, she wondered? Any kind of book nicker? But she'd only nicked an unpublished book. Surely that didn't count, did it? Not as much? But what if?

Maggie sat down at the table as Mary carefully towel dried her fancy plates.

"Seen Peter lately?" Mary asked pleadingly.

"Oh, Mum you've got to forget about Petey."

"Why? He's a good man. He'll forgive you for losing his papers. Won't he? He loves you. I know he does," Mary said.

"No, Mum. You don't know nothing."

"No? What do you mean, Mags?"

"Maybe I don't love him, huh? Why do you always think it's a one-way street? If a man loves you, it don't matter if you love him back, it's still a gig because maybe there's nothing else gonna come along."

"But you told me you loved him," she reminded Maggie.

"Well, that was then. Life goes on and it moves mighty fast. I should know. I spent the day speeding through stop signs!"

"In this rain?" Mary asked. "Why do I get the feeling you're up to something?"

"You've thought that since I was five," Maggie replied.

"Because you've always been up to your neck in something, that's why!"

Maggie stormed out. Things were barely beginning to pick up speed and she could feel the vibrations of the tracks, or was that only her teeth grinding?

* * *

The days seemed eternal and ever so gray for Peter, even when it wasn't raining. He'd become numb from worrying about Maggie. He still harbored a notion that they could one day work things out, but he couldn't reach her. She'd changed her phone number and never came around at the library. Peter was sure that Maggie thought he was angry for losing his manuscript, and that was why she'd become invisible.

With his gray shirt buttoned up tight, Peter sat at the breakfast table looking morose. Mrs. Chapman put his rack of toast in front of him and poured his tea.

"She never comes by the library. I look for her every day, but she's never there… never."

"No?" Mrs. Chapman asked. But what could she have said? Still, she'd long felt like Peter's mum in a way. "I'm so sorry for what happened."

"She didn't mean to lose my novel. Did she?"

"I know Alice is working hard retyping it. She said some of the pages were smudged from the carbons, but she's slowly getting through them. You know you can always depend on Alice, don't you, dear?"

"Yes," Peter replied. "Alice is always there, always good."

* * *

Despite the fact she didn't accomplish much, Mary still went to Louisa's three times a week. She let herself in and went about looking for something to keep her busy to earn the pound Louisa always put out for her.

Mary glanced into Louisa's silver cabinet and saw that every piece was gleaming.

"Looks like I have it all polished up, Louisa. I might have to pull out a dust cloth one day just to earn my wages!"

"Nonsense, Mary. Harold left me a pile of money, and there's nothing to do with it but spend it. Unless you can help me figure out a way to take it with me. I'll leave some extra on the table so you can help with that. Now, sit down so we can start discussing what we want for lunch. Shouldn't that take most of the morning, given we can never agree on anything."

Mary laughed and sat down and pulled out her knitting.

"Mary, you've been teaching me to knit for weeks now. Don't you think I'm getting a wee bit better?"

"No, Louisa. There's no worse knitter in London!"

"But look…"

Louisa held up her sweater but seemed perplexed at what she'd just discovered. It had two sleeves—one near the side, one mostly on the back, and an arm hole still waiting for the third sleeve.

"Oh, dear. I forgot how many sleeves I was going to put in."

"It tends to be only two, dear. That's tradition. You see? That's what I mean," Mary said. "Your sweater wouldn't make a good tea cozy."

"No? Wait! What about a tea cozy for a teapot with three spouts," Louisa declared, as though she'd somehow saved herself. "They're making them now, you know."

"No, they're not, Louisa, except in your head after its been fueled with two gins. Why would anyone want a teapot with three spouts?"

"To pour three cups of tea at once!" Louisa earnestly declared. "It's a good way to save time. Isn't it?"

"Nope, but good try," Mary said.

"Well, anyway, it's all your fault," Louisa added,

"Mine, you say?"

"I started this sweater the day we finished off the gin and found a bottle of wine that needed drinking before it got too old. You know, they say that a bottle of wine that sits around too long is likely to get more expensive."

"I know what you're doing," Mary said.

"Doing?" Louisa said.

"You're changing the subject from your sweater with three armholes. It was two bottles, dear. Each one over ten years old. But I can't count bottles any better than you can count sleeve holes. Got any more gin?"

"I'll go open another," Louisa said. "Then it won't matter how many sleeves my tea cozy has, or for that matter, how many we have!"

Louisa got up to get the bottle.

"Wait, Louisa. If we go through another bottle, I'm libel to get sloppy and accuse you of being the best knitter in London!"

"Yes! Then I'll bring two bottles!" Louisa announced with a smile. "Think of what an incredible knitter I'll be by tea time!"

16

LATE OR NOT, Maggie still always showed up. Well, nearly that is. Many mornings her thoughts were traveling to destinations other than the makeup counter. She dashed into Selfridges late, but Ann had been unable to cover for her this time. Bulldog had been sniffing around and growling louder and louder of late. She came to realize that Maggie's sales book had lots of sales, despite the fact she was seldom seen on the floor. Her big lipstick sales were not going to save her this time.

Maggie hid her umbrella behind the counter and grabbed a mirror to check her lipstick.

"Has Bulldog made her rounds yet?"

"Yes," Ann said. "She has, and she's waiting for you in her office."

"She is? Is she going to fire me?"

"I think so," Ann replied.

Maggie looked resolved. She knew there was no point in fighting for her job. She'd used every trick in the book to stay on the payroll as long as she could. Resigned to her fate, Maggie simply grabbed her umbrella to leave.

"Tell Bulldog I went shopping," Maggie whispered before putting on a smile that quickly fell off.

"Shopping?" Ann whispered. "She thinks that's all you do, anyway."

"Well, this is a store, isn't it?!" Maggie said. "I'll be seeing you, Annie."

"Good luck, Maggie!"

Maggie walked out with her head hung low. To face the world out there, she tried to crank up her chin, but it kept falling back down. Yes, Maggie's mood was dragging the ground that morning.

She went down into the tube station and stood there waiting for a train, but when she opened her purse for the fare, she found she hadn't a penny. Well, walking home gave her plenty of time to cry out her pain.

Back at the flat, Maggie hoped she could hide away until she'd worked out a story to tell her mum that she'd been made redundant and therefore there'd be no weekly paycheck coming in. She walked in and looked about the place.

"Mum? You home?"

But everything was quiet. Mary typically sang or hummed to herself as she did her housework. Where was she? Maggie slept in the bedroom and Mary on the sofa. There, her blankets were nicely folded and stacked.

About then, Maggie heard the key unlock the door. In came Mary in her housekeeper's dress and her pail of brushes she'd brought back from Louisa's as they were never used.

Mary gasped. She'd not wanted her daughter to know she'd been doing housework as she knew it had always been important to Maggie that she'd somehow take care of them.

"Mags, why are you home this time of day?"

Mary put her pail down. Maggie looked at it sitting there next to Mary's worn shoes.

"Mum, what's that?" she asked.

"You know what it is."

"I told you I'd take care of us," Maggie said. Despite being all cried-out, a tear still fell down her cheek.

"It's alright," Mary said. "Just going over to Louisa's to give her a hand now and again."

"Mrs. Harold? On the tube, by yourself? That's all the way out to Maresfield Gardens."

"Why are you crying?" Mary asked. "Sit down here and I'll make us a pot of tea."

"I don't want any tea."

"Well, I do," Mary said. "Look!"

Mary pulled out a pound.

"A whole pound!" Mary exclaimed. "Nothing to worry over. Me and Louisa, we're old friends. We talk, I pretend to do this and that, and then we have tea, a gin, and talk some more. Soon then we're hungry for lunch."

"Whatever do you talk about?" Maggie asked before taking a seat at the table as Mary put the kettle on for tea.

"Mostly you."

"Me? Why would that rich lady care about me?"

"Maggie, dear. When did you get to be so hard?"

"Maybe when I went around London with my mum lugging her pails and rags when I should have been in school."

"I want to do it. I enjoy being with Louisa. We're two near to being old ladies who have more in common than you'd think."

"You couldn't have anything in common!"

"No? If you only knew," Mary said.

"Knew what?" Maggie asked.

"Why are you home so early?"

"Mum, they let me go this morning. I walked around all afternoon because I didn't want to tell you…" Maggie started crying all over again. "… until I had to."

"Dear, you got fired, not charged with some awful crime," Mary said. "Aren't you glad I made enough to pay the electric?"

Mary kissed Maggie on the forehead and dabbed her tears with her tea cloth.

"We'll be fine. No worse than what it was for us during the war," Mary said.

"No, Mum. We've never been fine and it's never going to be unless I figure out something."

Maggie glanced at Mary's old bucket of brushes.

"Maggie, you were so happy when you were with Peter. What's happened to change that? Is there something you're not telling me?"

Maggie got up and left the room.

The following day Maggie arose late. Had no reason not to. She and her mum tried to avoid one another in the kitchen as there was too much tension, and talking about it wasn't going to fix a thing. Maggie again had no work and still she was conflicted because Mary was out there cleaning houses. She felt she'd let her mum down because she couldn't take care of her. But then again, things can happen and so often do.

Finally Mary broke the cold silence.

"There was a call this morning, dear."

"A call? Who was it, Mum?"

"Sandra. She wants you to come by the office. Is it about a job, do you think?"

Maggie's misery quickly fell away.

"Maybe, Mum. Maybe."

Maggie kissed Mary's cheek.

"I told you we'd get by!" Mary said.

"I know, Mum. I should listen to you. Some days I just can't see how things will ever work out for us and I can't get past it."

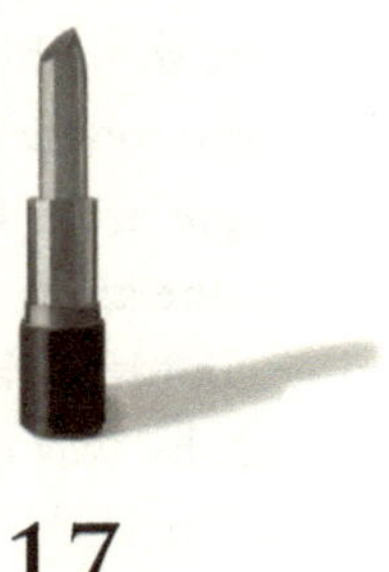

17

T HE FOLLOWING MONDAY, Maggie got up early for the appointment at the agency. She'd been asked to arrive at ten o'clock as Brandon seldom showed up earlier. Sandra didn't say why he'd requested the meeting. By chance, was it because he'd discovered her secret? It lingered in her thoughts as she readied her things, Maggie wondering if he would ask if she'd written the novel before or after she'd learned to read and write. *Anything is possible*, she heard that old familiar voice carp.

After pulling out her best outfit, she spent an hour arranging her hair, and nearly as long putting her make up on. For just the right touch, she applied a couple of coats of lipstick for good luck, and with high hopes, headed off. Well, maybe with only a sliver of hope. Had she really just heard

Joan Crawford telling her to chin up?

Thankfully, it hadn't rained that morning. It seemed to Maggie that it had been for days, so the sunshine was a good omen, although she didn't quite know for what. Still, she thought, her hair wouldn't be frizzed when she got there, and that was good.

Maggie arrived early to find Sandra at her post guarding against those claiming they were near to being famous writers only waiting to be discovered by some lucky agent.

Sandra actually seemed nice that morning, Maggie thought. But was that a good sign, or merely an act of mercy?

"He's waiting for you in there," she said.

"Waiting? But I'm not late."

"No, it's a sign," Sandra said.

With those words, Maggie felt her stomach flip-flop. Yep, that clearly meant her gig was already up as he had to know everything. Surely he was about to tell her off for wasting his time! He'd not sent a letter because he knew she'd never be able to read it, and so her thoughts rambled on.

"Good or bad?" Maggie finally stammered.

Sandra laughed and still did not lose her smile. *So, what does that grin really mean*, Maggie wondered?

"He doesn't ask writers in to deliver bad news. I get to ring up with that," Sandra said.

"I bet you're good at it, too." Maggie added.

Sandra smiled anyway and gestured to Brandon's door.

Maggie took a deep breath, and with chin up, probably like a movie star making her grand entrance at her premier, breezed in.

Brandon, who seemed even more handsome than when Maggie had met him, stood to greet her. Had he really grown an inch or two taller? Still, she halfway expected him to ask her who she really was and again why she said she was a writer? But he didn't. Nope. With a big smile, he motioned for her to take a seat. *Isn't that a good sign?* Maggie's thoughts were bouncing around in her head so loud Brandon surely heard the clanking.

"Miss Holiday, so good to see you again!"

He couldn't stop smiling.

"Maggie. My friends call me Maggie."

"Maggie, sure. But for an author, I like your real name better. Olivia Holiday has a ring to it. Like a movie star's, don't you think?"

Well, she did, didn't she?

As the conversation progressed, Maggie quickly realized that she and

Brandon were on the same page, even if it was one she'd neither written nor could read.

"Yes, Maggie, I would be delighted to represent you. Your novel is one of the most exciting things I've come across in a long time."

A tear came to Maggie's eye. She hoped Brandon didn't notice, and dabbed at her eyes as though a spec of dust had invaded.

"You read it? I mean it's very long isn't it?" she asked, struggling to be nonchalant.

"Usually I read a chapter or two and know if a writer has what it takes. I knew after the first two or three pages that you're an incredible talent. I read the entire novel over the weekend. Couldn't put it down."

Maggie sat back in her chair and took a deep breath. It suddenly occurred to her that she was truly in the race now! But where was she off to? She'd be pondering this question in the days and weeks ahead. Yep, the headaches were about to come in bundles.

18

AFTER SHELVING HUNDREDS of books that day, or so it seemed, Peter headed home. Because of the rain, he decided to spend a coin and use the tube. Saving his only pair of shoes was surely worth the ten pence. On the train, he glanced up and down the rows of seats to see if by chance his manuscript would be laying there. Like maybe under a seat were Maggie had forgotten it. But it wasn't a maybe that Peter was really looking for her. *Well, that's the way a writer's imagination works at times,* he thought. Fantasies and hopes waxing high, Peter knew that nothing was ever left on the tube that long. Still things can happen and it's all part of the poetry of life. In fact, it's the engine that drives it.

Back at Mrs. Chapman's, he went upstairs and put a tin of soup on his hotplate and unbuttoned his very buttoned up shirt. Then, as he shifted his things, he noticed a note from Alice. Maybe she'd slipped it under his door while he was putting his stuff away.

"Peter! Finished! Mum and I want to celebrate your new beginning. Come down for supper about seven!"

Peter checked his watch.

"I'm late!" he announced to the handsome man gazing back from the mirror next to his door.

Peter patted down his damp hair, buttoned his shirt up again, and headed downstairs. There, at his usual place, waited his manuscript, all perfectly typed as only Alice could do.

"My novel! It's come back to me!"

Peter took a deep breath and grabbed his manuscript and headed back upstairs again.

"Where are you going?" Mrs. Chapman asked.

"Don't know," he responded. With a sigh of relief, he plopped back down in his chair.

Alice was happy, too. She'd not seen such a smile on Peter's face for weeks.

Then, Peter noticed that Alice was nicely dressed.

"Alice, is your hair different?"

"Doesn't it look pretty?" Mrs. Chapman asked.

"Yeah, what should I do now?" he asked.

Alice looked at her mum.

"Do?" Alice asked.

"For the second time, it's all done! My novel! Who gets to live twice?" Well, things happen.

"Do you still want Fred to read it?" Alice asked.

"Do you think he'll want to?"

"I'll take it in myself," she promised, "and never once let it out of my sight!"

"Not like that other one!" Mrs. Chapman added.

"Thanks, Alice. You're so sweet to me."

"That's my daughter! And an excellent typist!"

* * *

Days went by, and still Maggie hadn't heard from Brandon. She paced about the flat while Mary knitted and watched her daughter seemingly unravel at times.

"Mags, I don't understand. If you have a new job, why aren't you at work?" Mary asked.

"I don't start until I start, Mum."

"Oh, I see," Mary replied, but really didn't. Still, Maggie seemed so tense she let it go.

Well, the call came that afternoon. Brandon summoned Maggie for a luncheon meeting for the following week. When the day came, Maggie woke up early wondering if Brandon would remember what she'd worn the first time he met her. Since he might, and because she had only one smart outfit, she decided to do her hair up differently. Then, she hoped, he'd think she looked different no matter the similarity of her exactly the same outfits. Mary watched on as Maggie gazed in the mirror and suggested her daughter wear a string of pearls. She pulled out of her drawer a string of pearls that kind of looked like pearls.

"It always makes a woman's face glow, and they never notice anything else," she said. "And who can tell plastic ones from real, hey?"

Well, it sounded good. *What the hell,* Maggie thought. They had to be good luck if her mum treasured them, real or not.

Maggie was more than anxious for this luncheon and wondered if she'd end up saying something that might blow her gig, or simply that Brandon might still come to decide she wasn't really an author he should bother with; after all, she wasn't an author, period. Maggie knew Brandon was a smart guy; Sandra had told her so repeatedly. Yet her thoughts seemed to wander in a different direction. Yep, like what if she was even smarter? Why not? Yeah, whose rules was she playing by now? Like Maggie always told herself, whatever comes up, I'll get around it.

She met Brandon in a posh restaurant, the likes of which she'd never been to. It was off the lobby of a grand hotel. The doorman pointed her in the direction of the restaurant.

"Blimey, I hope he's paying…" she yammered to herself before grabbing her lipstick for another quick coat as she swept in.

As soon as Brandon noticed her, he stood and smiled. *Well,* Maggie thought, *whatever the agenda, it was unlikely to be bad news with that toothy grin.*

"Miss Holiday, good to see you!"

A waiter pulled the chair out for her. Maggie thought Brandon only seemed to get more handsome. Perhaps it was reading her novel that did it but then how could that even be given Peter had written it? Well, anyway… She needed a drink to calm her thoughts before they pushed their way out her ears. One more deep breath was called for.

Soon the waiter returned with a tray of martinis.

"Last week I invited publishers to make offers," Brandon announced.

"Offers of money?" Maggie took a another gulp of her martini.

He chuckled.

"I love your humor. So, if they're as impressed as I am with your talent, we may be talking big advance."

Maggie looked perplexed.

"What do I have to advance again?" she asked and followed Brandon's smile with a bit of one herself wondering if smiling pretty was part of the protocol at these author luncheons? And Brandon, she was beginning to think, was sure pretty.

"Funny. I love it! So, we're headed for big money if we handle our cards right, and that's my job. I'll take care of everything!"

"Everything?" she asked.

"Just leave it to me!" he reiterated. "I'm the best in the business!"

Maggie liked the sound of that. Yep, taking care of everything surely meant the kitchen cupboards might soon be filled with something other than emptiness. That was a pleasant thought that her mum could also relate to. Like she'd told Mary, she'd take care of them, come hell or high water. Well, there would be days of near drowning in those high waters but that was yet to come.

After a few smiles back and forth, the waiter brought another round of drinks and handed them menus.

"I can't wait to tell Mum. She loved it when I read it to her by candlelight."

Did she really say that? Actually, what she meant was that Mary loved Peter's reading of his own novel. But as Maggie always said, "a book is a book is a book." Why get bogged down with reading the fine print one can't read anyway?

"Good! Excellent," he said. "Keep practicing as the publisher will want you to do readings of your novel. It will be in the contract."

Maggie put her martini glass down looking a bit stunned.

"What? Read it? Myself? In public?" Maggie asked.

Maggie quickly gulped her drink to the finish.

"No need to be reticent. All writers do staged readings. You'll love it. The audience looking up at you as you carry them along on the dreamscapes you're so good at painting in your writing."

"Staged, you say? Like reading up on a stage?"

"Sure. You'll be able to see people in their seats smiling up at you, I'm sure." He smiled again to show her what it might look like. "You're an incredible writer with a quirky sense of humor and should be so celebrated and I'll be the one to make it happen. Just leave it to me."

And why not? she wondered, and thought he had teeth like a movie star.

"I love your humor," he said again. "Most of my writers are stuffy old men with no sense of humor. You're truly a delight and your public will love you as much as they love your writing."

Maggie left the two-martini luncheon having eaten little and feeling a bit light-headed. She walked out wondering what it would feel like being up on a stage, people's eyes focused on her, and then she'd open the book, her book, but nothing would come out of her mouth because she couldn't read? Wait a minute! *What's going wrong here*, she wondered? Well now. The train was taking on speed still no one had yet asked her for her ticket. But was that really a good sign or some kind of freak omission? Time would tell, if she could only get herself that far.

"Read it?" she yammered to herself. "Did he say read it? Well, I'll get around it, or, I guess, they'll burn me at the stake like a witch!"

Maggie's mum was delighted to hear that her daughter had a job, which she more or less described. Well, actually on the less side of things. Only a comment or two about working in an office with what sounded like a real handsome and dashing man. Still, at least they could plan on eating again, and that delighted them both.

As the book deal had yet been finalized, Brandon had given her a hefty twenty-pound advance against royalties, which Maggie happily took along on a shopping spree. There's something about having money in your purse when out shopping that makes it all the more enjoyable. She hoped she might cross paths with Bulldog Livingston, but was even more pleased to see Ann. She ran into her with bags of things she'd just purchased.

"Wow!" Ann exclaimed. "You've married your rich writer or have a great new job!"

"I'm going to a party Saturday night. You know, the kind famous writers go to."

"With Peter?"

"No, with a guy I think will be my new boyfriend," Maggie said with a twinkle in her eye.

She was riding high for a change, and it sure felt good. *Why shouldn't it?* she asked herself.

But at home, Maggie's mum tended to stay grounded, even when her daughter was flying high reaching for those helter-skelter dreams of hers.

Maggie pulled out her fancy new clothes and shoes and laid them over the sofa for viewing. Mary was taken back. *Either Mags has won a lottery or robbed a bank*, she thought. Or perhaps been discovered by Hollywood. Well, had to be a no on that one as the Atlantic Ocean had a word or two to put on that thought given what Maggie had left in her purse wouldn't buy even a row boat. Oh, well. What does it matter which way you're headed so long as you get there?

"Where's all the money coming from?" Mary asked as she looked over Maggie's many purchases.

"Mum, I told you I have a new job."

"Doing what? Going to fancy lunches and shopping all afternoon? And who gets paid before they even start? You haven't gone into no office all week."

Having survived the war when everything was rationed, Mary never went shopping at fancy stores for new clothes. Folks on their street just didn't do that. One bought cast offs at the church bizarre or farmers' market and just made do.

"It's really important to dress the part. Yes? When have you ever seen the Queen wearing castoffs?"

Maggie pulled out a cocktail dress and held it up to herself. It was a blue-green peacock color that shimmered in the light.

"I've never seen such a beautiful frock," Mary said.

Maggie kissed her cheek.

"Don't worry, Mum. It's going to be good for us for a change! Like I promised, hey?"

Still, Mary wondered. Dreams can quickly stack up so high on feathery clouds that they end up pouring rain. How could Mary have known that Maggie's train had already taken off and was taking on speed right towards the abyss? But anyway, who cared? Nope, not Maggie. There wasn't time to fuss about such things and she was already dressed the part and simply didn't concern herself with unpleasant realities. That was all left behind somewhere in her past lives. Anyway, even better days were only up the tracks. Weren't they? *Well, it's all in how I play my cards,* Maggie kept reminding herself.

19

T HE FOLLOWING WEEK, Brandon escorted the newly-created Miss Holiday to a meeting at the publisher's office. The one that Brandon had told her was likely to offer the biggest advance for the novel. Maggie had been nervous the entire week before and couldn't do much more than pace the flat, which only made Mary nervous alongside her.

"I don't understand why you don't go to work if you have a new job?" Mary asked again, but this time expected a real answer.

"They're getting my office ready," was all Maggie could come up with. But Mary was skeptical. Something seemed amiss. What woman had her own office anyway?

Finally, the day came for the big meeting at the publishing house. Maggie was dressed, well, like a movie star. She wondered if her dress was so tight the publishers might to see her stomach doing somersaults? That possible? She pulled out of her wardrobe a big handbag she'd hold at her waist just in case.

Brandon picked her up in the big black sedan.

"Remember, don't say a word unless you have to. Just nod and smile," Brandon directed his client. "We'll sort the particulars later."

"Ah, smile and…? Does it matter the order?"

Brandon snickered.

"Nothing to be nervous about. Only a room full of book editors. We have them by the, well, you know."

She did and spoke plain English.

"By the bollocks?"

"You read my mind," Brandon replied. "They all want your novel to be as successful. After all, they aim to see their advance paid back."

"Advance? How much of an advance?"

"We'll get to that," he said. "Just let me hammer out the details for the best deal."

Maggie entered the mahogany paneled boardroom, closely followed by Brandon. He appeared to know everyone and nodded or shook their hands as Maggie smiled, and then smiled even more to make her point.

"Miss Holiday, I'm delighted to meet you," one of the suit men said.

Maggie nodded and smiled. She was quick to get the hang of things.

"We love your first book. Can't wait to read the second," another suit added.

Did he say second? As in second novel, Maggie wondered? That very comment brought the first somersault of the morning. She clutched her big bag for comfort but there were more to come.

"Second… book?" Maggie asked Brandon in a whisper.

"You signed a two-book deal," he whispered back. "I'll catch you up on it later."

With those words, "two books, Maggie suddenly felt a bit dizzy. Maybe as when a train hurls around a corner too fast! Can trains flip over on their heads? That's where Maggie felt herself headed. Her stomach did another somersault so she clutched her big bag all the tighter and wondered how far away her mum could be.

"That's how much confidence we have in your talent, Miss Holiday," the first suit man added.

Maggie nodded but this time couldn't seem to work up even a tiny grin.

"They're talking about a book tour from coast to coast," Brandon added.

"But who reads books at the sea?" Maggie let slip out. She realized it sounded ridiculous but couldn't take it back and so smiled as though it was merely a joke. All she could imagine was standing on a sandy beach, with book in hand looking about for one of the sunbathers to read for her while others made sandcastles with their beach pails.

Well, the publishers laughed all the same, didn't they? Like Brandon said, they all seemed to be stuffy old men who probably only liked reading sales figures. Nothing else truly mattered. Still, what was that sound in her ear? *Could it possibly be a ticking bomb,* she wondered? Or her teeth grinding all the louder? Maggie nodded and smiled, and then smiled again for good measure. Still she felt growing apprehension as Brandon sped up her little train ride that he'd seemingly jumped aboard.

At that, Brandon stood and nodded to all the suits and offered his arm to escort Maggie from the room.

Brandon was delighted with her performance that morning. Still, Maggie couldn't help but wonder if smiling and nodding at the gallows would save her neck. Her palms were getting sweaty with that ever redundant vision of the executioner shaking his head suggesting not a chance. That ax as sharp as it looks? Maggie's thoughts were breathing heavy.

As they walked to lunch after the meeting, Brandon held on tightly to Maggie. Of course, he did. She was a good investment, and he wouldn't want her to get run down by a lorry until after she'd written that second novel. And then, who knows how many novels after that? Maggie wasn't good at counting so it hardly mattered in the long run.

"You were excellent. Incredible!" he said again.

"How? I didn't open my mouth," she replied, loosening Brandon's clutch.

"And you did it brilliantly. Listen, I want you to meet some people, important people."

Maggie wondered how many 'important people' she'd already met and how many more were to come? Her face was getting a bit smile-weary.

"Why? They want me to read to them? Or just watch me nod and smile?"

"It's all about connecting to the right people who can make a difference for us," he replied.

"Us?" she asked.

"Book sales! That's what keeps the ship afloat! Don't worry yourself.
We're almost there."

And the train screeched ahead into the blurry depths of Maggie, er,
ah, Olivia Holiday's, dreams.

20

ALICE WENT TO the office early most days to start opening agency mail. But that morning, she had a special task. She'd brought Peter's retyped novel manuscript and aimed to drop it, or rather situate it at the top of Fred's read stack. But Fred had arrived early that morning. What was she going to do? She opened a few envelopes and then pretended she'd just opened the one with Peter's novel enclosed and took it into Fred's office.

"This is the best writing we've ever received. Truly, Fred."

But Fred was preoccupied with his stack to get through.

"Put it on the bottom over there," he said without a glance her way.

"Okay, on the bottom," she replied knowing that clearly meant Fred would not get to it for days or even weeks. Never?

So, after shuffling through the papers on Fred's desk like an actress arranging her props, she placed Peter's manuscript at the top of Fred's morning readings.

Mission accomplished, Alice smiled and headed back to her desk.

* * *

Brandon told Maggie her book contract was all in order and that things were rolling along as planned. He would, he informed her once again, take care of everything, and reminded her that he was successful in launching talented new writers. The very words felt good to Maggie. She wasn't going to send them packing. Yes, she thought, she'd made the right decision dropping in on the poshest agency she could ever have conjured an image of. *Was she creeping closer to Hollywood?* was her passing thought. Well, maybe and maybe not. One can't look anywhere but straight ahead when balancing on a tightrope that's a bit too close to the sun. Joan Crawford told her to just keep going and smile harder when the road, or tracks got bumpy. She know Brandon?

The weeks sped by and so did all the commotion about Maggie's book. Yes, her readers loved it and her! Brandon had planned a big author's coming out party, where she'd wear her new shimmering peacock-colored cocktail dress. It still worried Maggie how many people might ask her, let us say 'awkward' questions. Like perhaps what was it like being a writer who couldn't write… or read? Still, she reminded herself that whatever came up she'd get around it. She'd long survived by swerving from reality. Most of the time it work? Yeah? Why not this time, or the next, and then the one after that, hey? But then again, how many times would she have to tell herself this before she actually believed it? Well, she wasn't any better at counting than she was at reading. No, counting all those broken dreams can get tangled for the brokenhearted. And did anyone really say broken hearts can be repaired? Maggie snickered at the notion. She'd been that way too many times to count.

As the car pulled curbside that evening, she glanced up at the fancy building and watched as a doorman, dressed like he'd come from some fancy hotel, opened the door for arriving guests.

Maggie stepped out of the black sedan and grasped Brandon's arm. Her nerves were clinging to him, too.

"Remember, it's Olivia tonight, not Maggie," he admonished. He'd told her that Maggie sounded like a cleaning woman's name. Well, why not, she wondered? Really? Both Maggie and Olivia agreed on that one. Who the hell cares? As long as there was free food in there it didn't matter, did it?

Inside, they headed up the fancy stairs to the flat above. She could hear the clinking of martini glasses and wondered if they really showed to meet her or for the free food? She pondered the many times during the war she and Mary would have walked across town for a free meal like the ones the church put out now and again. Now they were tossing invitations at her for simply being a brilliant writer, or so that's what Brandon kept telling her. Yeah, so again, who the hell cares? Not Maggie's stomach. She could smell the smoked salmon and caviar from the curb. Well, maybe.

The butler opened the door to the flat with a slight bow, as though Maggie were a baroness or something. Brandon didn't seem to notice him; he was already apprising the fancy people clinking fancy glasses in the drawing room that lay ahead.

"Smile. They'll love you," he whispered and plastered one on his own face as they entered.

Maggie took a deep breath and reminded herself that one slip and they'd all know she was no writer. But what if they should ask what she was reading these days? She needed a bit of hand-holding.

"What should I say?" she whispered to Brandon.

"Don't worry," he said. "They won't be asking for a speech. Just nod and smile, and then smile some more. They'll get the point quick enough."

Maggie was puzzled.

"What point?"

"That you're simply too important for chit-chat."

"Nod and smile?" she asked, and clutched Brandon's arm even tighter.

"Believe me, nothing they say is worth listening to," he said. "I've been to dozens of these parties; they're all dreadfully boring."

Maggie glanced over the posh room and noticed guests pause their cocktail chatter to observe her entrance. Like Brandon's, their faces were wall-to-wall smiles.

Maggie nodded and smiled right back at them and the chatter resumed. Her very presence brought a feeling of power that she'd never known the likes of before. Had she somewhere or somehow crossed the threshold of stardom and no one had enlighten her? Well, perhaps, but still not the finish line. There was more to come.

Soon, a waiter appeared out of nowhere with a tray of cocktails. Maggie shook her head 'no,' but then grabbed one in each hand. Brandon turned to position his back against the room and grabbed one of Maggie's drinks and returned it to the waiter's tray.

"Remember, we never have more than one drink at a reception," he whispered.

Still, Maggie wondered how many drinks it would take to calm her nerves? Probably enough to fill the room like a garden pool.

"I can remember 'one'; it's when I get past 'two' that I lose count," she said.

"That's why only one is best," Brandon reminded her.

Brandon always found Maggie's humor amusing. But still she wondered if he'd really heard her comment as her hand was shaking so badly her bracelets jingled. Yep, thoughts were buzzing her head like dive-bombers. The echo in her head was getting louder. Who would approach and ask her about her writing? What was she reading these days? *War and Peace* perhaps? Or maybe James Joyce's *Ulysses*, a book everyone had on a shelf, but no one ever read? She remembered Brandon making such comments and quickly salted them away for an evening like this. Still, she thought, she could always chat about the pictures she looked at over and over again in her movie star magazines.

"I love your humor. It's utterly delicious."

Maggie gulped her drink as Brandon led them through a room of brilliant smiles. She offered her hand to kiss, or rather shake as she nodded and smiled, but then started feeling sick to her stomach. Was the room really teetering? *Why do all these people seem to look like movie stars?* she wondered. And what if they all had housekeepers who were named Maggie?

21

Days passed and not a word from Fred about Peter's manuscript, so Alice decided she would drive the issue; after all, Peter was cute and held a special place in her scheme of things.

"Two more today manuscripts came in today!" Alice announced from her desk out front. "Have you read that really good one yet? The one from Peter Tinsley?"

"Haven't read any that were particularly good," he said.

Alice bound into Fred's office to see where Peter's was. Back there, she went through the pile that Fred had stacked, knocked over, re-stacked and, in frustration, finally shoved off his desk to that ever growing pile close to his feet.

Alice combed through the pile and pulled Peter's out.

"It's your next read," she said.

She opened Peter's manuscript to the first page and all but shoved it into Fred's hand.

"Here! This will make your day!" she said.

"How?" Fred's voice was full of frustration. "Have you sensed I may be drifting towards the embankment again? Don't worry. I'll never jump in on a day as cold as this! Remember, I hate cold water."

"I'm glad to hear it. I mean that you don't like cold water, so you'll be back tomorrow," Alice said with a smile.

Fred started to read Peter's work, and kept reading… and reading.

Late that morning, Alice slipped out for sandwiches. When she returned, Fred was standing in the door of his office looking as though someone had said it was his birthday after forgetting he still had them. Yep, his mood had flipped to thumbs up. Alice was taken back. She'd not seen that expression for a long time.

"Fred, what is it?"

"This one!"

He waved the manuscript as if it were a prize. Well, it was. He flipped back to the title page for the author's name.

"Peter Tinsley. Get this chap in as soon as possible," he said.

"I have him scheduled for tomorrow at twelve," Alice replied.

"How? You haven't even spoken to him."

"I'm simply remarkable. That's how," she said.

And Fred knew she was.

"Right! So is your writer friend. Why didn't you bring his work to my attention earlier?" he asked.

"He can take off from his job at lunchtime. I'll have him here, don't worry."

* * *

Well, Maggie was certainly on a roll. Brandon asked her to yet another one of those posh dinner parties. He mentioned it would be a big bash in a fancy London district. Just the kind that Maggie had come to enjoy over the past few weeks particularly as no one ever asked her about her writing. In fact, they only told her how incredible she was. So, who has a problem with that? Yes, her train was taking on speed and that made getting up mornings a delight as it was sure nice to mingle with the rich, beautiful and well-fed. Maybe like the movie stars did in Hollywood. Joan Crawford winked at the notion. Hadn't they long been on the same wavelength? Sure, acting like a star made you one. Well, didn't it? Perhaps, but only if one can stay in character when the the lights go off. Brandon told her to get especially dressed for that night. The big black sedan came for Cinderella at the prescribed time. Brandon would be joining her there.

The car pulled up to a fancy townhouse where outside everything appeared so white and polished. A liveried doorman admitted her like he recognized her on sight. Upstairs the room glittered and was thronged with some of the most beautiful people she'd ever seen. Brandon, wearing his dinner jacket, had already arrived and waited in the foyer. He took her arm, smiled big and escorted her on in. As soon as they walked into the drawing room the throng of guest went silent, and then applause erupted. *Whatever for,* Maggie wondered? *They like my new shade of lipstick?* Joan Crawford whispered in Maggie's thoughts for her to hang on tight and go along for the ride wherever it might take her. That was most of any gig anyway, wasn't it? Show up and smile and let them think whatever and wherever their fantasies might take them. Joan Crawford was renowned for holding on and she could do it with a big smile. Just ask her dear, dear friend, Betty Davis who was frequently right at Joan's backside. Well, with a knife that is. But do all rising stars have to watch for the knives to come, or is that only in the movies? That thought was bound to return to Maggie as things progressed in the weeks ahead.

Brandon drew Maggie close and whispered in her ear.

"Wanted to make it a surprise. You see, your incredible book has hit the top of the charts!"

"Charts? That the same as a map?" she asked and glanced out over those faces that looked remarkably like the same ones she'd seen in all the other receptions Brandon had escorted her to. Could these people be following her? Yeah, but was it only to watch her trip over herself and fall headfirst onto the executioner's block? Maybe…

Brandon thought her comment was only a joke. Yet, Maggie wasn't trying to be amusing. The news that she was suddenly a literary star had made her ill. Maybe about like the day they announced the war had been declared. It was all coming too fast and so were things starting to spin out of control? The train ride she'd been enjoying had in a wink become a roller-coaster. So what would they think of her now if she went and threw up on that hundred year old Persian carpet they were mingling about on?

"I think I need to get out of here. I can't breathe."

She grabbed onto Brandon as the room started to sway. Maggie turned white and looked as if she might vomit. How could the guests not have wondered what was going on? She had to exit fast.

"I need to go…"

"Go? What? Now? Why?" Brandon asked and then turned to give the room another one of his brilliant smiles. Yes, everything was just great his smile conveyed.

Well, maybe not this time. The room looked on.

"My mum is calling me."

"Huh? You're ill? Something you ate?"

"No, it's something I'm going to eat, and I know it isn't going down no matter how hard I choke on it."

"Choke on what? You haven't eaten anything. You never do!" Brandon became as heated as he could without making a scene.

"I'm leaving," she said and turned towards the door as the bewildered guests watched dumbfounded.

Brandon grabbed to brace Maggie for a quick exit.

"Sure. The car will be waiting downstairs."

Well, the silence was deadening on the trip back to Maggie's part of town. Brandon, annoyed as hell, bit his lip but kept his mouth shut as Maggie gazed out the window as if she was sure to be heading in the wrong direction. And she sure enough was. Yep, she'd been heading down the wrong way for weeks now.

He delivered her home, but Maggie wasn't interested in a goodnight kiss. She got out of Brandon's fancy car and headed upstairs to the flat without turning back to blow a kiss. Mary would be there for her. She was always there for her Mags.

In her room, Maggie pulled and tugged to get out of her cocktail dress and then tossed it on the floor as though it were an old bathrobe.

Soon, Mary appeared with a glass of warm milk.

"I heard you come in. Not feeling well?"

"Mum, you know hot milk makes me sick."

Still, Maggie grabbed the glass of milk and drank it down.

"What do you eat at all the fancy parties you go to?" Mary asked and took the glass so Maggie could finish undressing.

"I mostly never eat. I can't have food on my teeth when they come up to meet me."

"What's that? Who wants to meet you? And why?" Mary asked and sat on Maggie's bed waiting for the lowdown. "What's wrong? Look how thin you are."

"Who said anything was wrong? It's this new job. Mum, I don't know if I can make it. I keep hearing crashing noises in my head."

"Of course, you can. You've always made it. You always will, even if you don't do it the way they expect."

Maggie began to cry. She sat down on the bed and Mary patted her like a child needing comforting.

"Thanks, Mum. What would I do without you?"

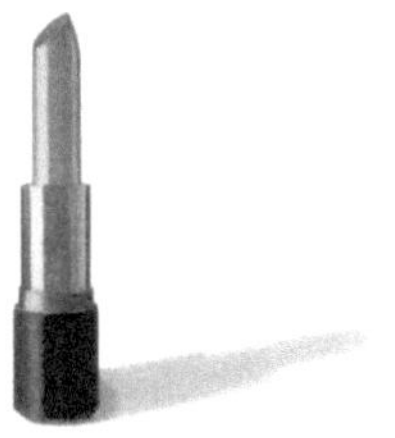

22

ALICE COULD NOT have been more excited. She'd saved Peter from manuscript purgatory in Fred's office, and couldn't wait to tell him.

Mrs. Chapman was preparing a nice dinner. Alice rang her up earlier and asked her to leave a note asking Peter to join them.

"Is he here yet?" Alice asked her mum the moment she came into the kitchen.

"No," Mrs. Chapman said as she took the boiled turnips out of the pot. "I hope your news for Peter is good. You know how sad he's been these last few weeks and he's lost weight, don't you think?"

At that moment, Peter walked in wet after getting caught in a downpour coming home.

"Peter, sit down. Alice is here!"

"I can see that, Mrs. Chapman."

"You're all wet," Alice said.

"I can see that, too." he said and laughed. "It was a heavy rain, but not blinding."

"Oh, Peter. I have great news. Fred wants to meet you."

"Why?" Peter asked, slumping into his seat like a wet rag. "Why?"

Alice was nearly beside herself with excitement.

"He likes your novel! I think he's going to help you find the right publisher."

"You mean he's already read it?" Peter asked grinning ear to ear.

"But I have to work at the library tomorrow," he replied, and brushed back the wet hair from his eyes.

"I know," Alice replied. "He'll meet you at your lunchtime. Just come! I'll have sandwiches there for you and Fred. You can eat while you chat about your novel."

Peter could hardly believe his ears.

"He read it? Isn't that a good sign?"

"Yes, Peter. He loves it!"

"Thanks, Alice. Thanks, Mrs. Chapman. I don't know if I'd want to be here if it weren't for you."

Peter smiled and headed upstairs.

"What did Peter mean by that? " Wouldn't want to be here"? Mrs. Chapman asked.

"He's an artist, Mum. Their hearts are wrapped up in their work. When it's gone, or stolen, as happened to Peter, their souls take a beating."

Upstairs, Peter washed his drab gray shirt so it would dry before morning. At exactly nine o'clock, he was back in his room, and never heard the couple in the next room jouncing the bed-springs.

* * *

The following Monday, after fleeing the big party, Maggie felt better. Perhaps the train that was seemingly hurling her towards the cliff had slowed a bit. Or perhaps she simply didn't care. After all, wasn't it all a done deal, no matter what was ultimately to happen? But then again, just what if no one ever caught on to her? Which way was the dice rolling? As Mary reminded her, she'd always gotten by somehow. Maggie got dressed and headed for the tube and off to Brandon's office, where it seemed Sandra may have been waiting for her.

"He seems upset," Sandra whispered the moment Maggie walked in.

"He's found out!" Maggie yammered under her breath. She could only have wondered if Brandon had finally figured out that she couldn't read the novel she'd written. Well, so to speak written. That was still the role she was playing on stage anyway. But hadn't it become Brandon's stage now?

"Pardon?" Sandra asked.

Maggie shook her head. She was unlikely to elaborate.

"Brandon's worried he's been pushing you too hard," Sandra said quietly and glanced over at Brandon's closed office door. "Don't let him do that! You know how ambitious he is."

Maggie nodded to everything Sandra said. She was being pushed too hard, and if she didn't play her cards right, circumstances might hurl her right over that jagged cliff. The one she kept seeing in her nightmares. Yes, the stakes were piling higher by the day. The stakes they burn witches and plagiarists on, that is.

"Just hang on! Everything will be good," Sandra said. "All authors have nerves. It's like stage fright. Sure, it is. But it never killed anyone."

Yeah, and anyway, how many times can one be beheaded, Maggie wondered? *And do they keep the Tower open late for such events?*

"Well, there's always a first time."

Maggie's voice had suddenly taken on the blunt edge of one resigned to catastrophe. Was it to be her fate, or could she keep events turned her way? Seeing Mary's old cleaning pail and brushes under the table that morning helped her work that out in her head. She had to do it for her mum; hold on for as long as she could. But then what?

"Go on in. He's expecting you."

Maggie slipped off her fancy coat—the one Ann had helped her select at Selfridges—tossed it over the chair, and went in.

Brandon stood to greet his star author.

"Olivia, good to see you! Did you get some rest over the weekend?"

"No. I was working on the second novel. Came up with the title but couldn't write it down. So, I just skipped the second novel and started the third. It's about a terribly desperate girl who throws herself on the train tacks when she learns her library books are overdue."

"Right…," was all Brandon could say. "Didn't get enough sleep, hey?" He motioned for Maggie to take a seat. "It's all my fault, you know."

"What is?" Maggie asked. "Me not sleeping?"

Brandon handed her his usual chuckle.

"You're a newly published author." And Brandon said that looking sincere. "I understand that kind of stress. This kind of success too early is never good a thing. It just happens so rarely. But don't worry. We're going to slow things down. As always, you can count on me to handle everything so not to worry. You know that."

The comment made Maggie wonder how slow things were for those sentenced to prison for fraud where a single day might feel like a decade or two? She gave Brandon a nod but left the smile part out.

23

I
T WAS A big day for Peter—perhaps the biggest yet in his life. He was early, yes, early to the library that morning. There was a spring in his step, and he simply couldn't slow it down and didn't want to. It was the beginning of more than just a new day; even reminded him of the day they announced the war was over. Better days were surely ahead! Weren't they? Sure, even as he no longer had someone special to share his dreams of being a published novelist with as Maggie was now history to him.

Peter left the library for Fred's office at noon sharp. He'd decided to spend some coin and use the tube as he didn't want his gray shirt to wrinkle from the drizzle. Well, Fred was hardly a fashion god, was he?

He went into the agency office and was welcomed by Alice's smile. That was a good sign as he knew she always took on a serious countenance when things weren't going well.

"Peter, you're here!"

"Yes. Why? Did I get the wrong time?"

"No, of course not," Alice replied. "I'm just excited about you meeting Fred. He's in there, waiting."

Alice motioned for Peter to join Fred in his office. Fred stood to shake his hand and pointed to a chair across from his desk. Fred's office was piled everywhere with stacks of papers, books, and manuscripts.

Fred simply pushed the pile closest off his desk and onto the floor, where it landed on the other piles.

They'd barely shaken hands when Alice appeared with sandwiches she'd picked up earlier. She handed one to Fred and the other to Peter along with a wink. Clearly, things were going as Alice would wish. That was a good sign.

"Is this your first novel?" Fred asked.

"Well, I wrote another one long ago. But I'd probably get arrested if I let anyone read it."

"Think nothing of it. First novels are seldom good," Fred said. "But this one that Alice drew my attention to is truly good. I would like to represent you. In fact, Alice insists that I do."

Fred twisted his neck over to see if Alice had overheard. From her desk, she smiled and kept shuffling through her stack of agency mail keeping her ear still cocked.

Fred and Peter talked and talked about his work, and which publishers would be most likely interested in publishing it. All the excitement was too much for Peter. He finally took a big bite of his sandwich, long after Fred had finished his, and got up to leave.

"I have to go back to the library," he said.

"Take your sandwich with you, Peter."

Sandwich in hand, Peter left passing Alice's desk.

"You've always been good to me." His smile seemed to have a long pause in it—as long as the gleam in his eyes.

Alice couldn't love Peter any more than she did that bright afternoon. His smile was only one of the reasons.

* * *

Maggie didn't want Mary to go out and clean houses. Well, that is she didn't want Mary to have to. She wanted to be able to care for her mum. But things happen, and one never knows at what corner they will, yet the bills still must be settled.

Mary had a great friend in Louisa even as their lives had traveled along different paths; Louisa led the life of a privileged woman, and Mary struggled to keep her and Maggie afloat. Despite all the miles Louisa and Mary had not shared during the war years, they were united by past dreams, laughs, and something else they'd shared but never talked about, even after a gin and tonic or two… or three.

"When did we meet, Mary?"

"If we go back that far, we'll be confessing our true age." Louisa said. "I know it was in boarding school, wasn't it?"

"What I remember was, you were pretty and all the boys loved you," Mary said.

"But you still got them all" Louisa said. "Doesn't that mean you were the prettiest?"

"I did? Get them all, I mean?"

"You got Harold, didn't you?"

"If I did, I never even noticed. How's that for you?" Mary said. "And you, Louisa. Aren't you Mrs. Harold?"

* * *

The traffic was heavy in South Kensington as Brandon and Maggie headed off. They'd had supper by candlelight in a nice place. Maggie thought he was delivering her to her flat, but he wasn't. As they sped through the city, she kept peering out the window but didn't recognize where they were.

"Are we lost? Where are we going?" she asked.

The driver seemed to know where he was taking them. Brandon smiled as the car pulled curbside. He got out and Maggie followed. Standing at the curb, Brandon gestured to the looming white townhouse that stood in front of them.

"Well, this is it!" he declared. "What do you think?"

"This is what?" she asked and glanced up and down the elegant street.

Brandon gestured to the grand door up the steps with pots of well-tended flowering plants flanking it. He motioned for her to follow him. They entered an elegant foyer with a large crystal chandelier hanging from two stories above.

"Is this a hotel?" she asked. "Where is everyone?"

Brandon smiled.

"It's my parents' place. They have another one in Paris. That's where they spend most of their time. They're over there now and probably won't return to London until opera season."

"Are you even kidding?" Maggie looked about with amazement. "Only one family lives here, or actually doesn't live here? Golly!"

"Come, I'll show you around," Brandon said and took her hand to lead her in. "It's four floors up and down and below not including this and that."

From the foyer, Brandon swung open French doors to the principle drawing room. There had to have been three sofas with pairs of French chairs saddled up close. Think of the parties! The tables were covered with expensive looking *objects de lux* and photos in fancy frames.

"I've never seen such a beautiful room. What am I saying? Never been in one to see!"

Maggie was hesitant to go in.

"My mum spent more than a year redecorating this room alone. She uses the same decorators that work at the palace."

"No lie?"

Maggie strolled over to a large French-style *bureau plat* and picked up a photo of Brandon as a child.

"This you?" she asked.

Brandon nodded.

"I know, I was cute back then. Well, you see what working too hard does to a man."

"Yeah, it makes you big, and apparently rich."

Brandon chuckled, but Maggie remained silent. He saw how ill-at-ease she was, and pulled her close.

"Olivia, we could have a fabulous life."

"We?" she asked. "It sort of looks like you're already there."

"With your talent and my management, you could be the biggest writer to come along in years. We're talking big money."

"What do you mean? I don't get the 'we' part of it."

"Just as I knew you'd be big, real big, I knew that I'd come to have strong feelings for you."

"Strong feelings?"

"Whatever you want to call it. Your wit makes me tingle and giggle," he said a wee bit unconvincingly.

"Funny, I've never heard you giggle."

Maggie looked about the grand room again.

"Nope, never."

"It's all inside of me. For now, anyway…" he strangely said.

He took Maggie's hand and kissed it.

"Come, I'll show you the library."

But she pulled away. Brandon was taken back and had that "what did I say?" puzzled look. His charm always worked. Didn't it? He reached to kiss her hand again, figuring that was a good starting place, but again she pulled back.

"No, I guess I'm feeling all booked up tonight."

Brandon chuckled, but it was forced. He expected Maggie to spend the night and confirmed his desires when he bent to kiss her on the mouth. But Maggie shook her head 'no', turned and walked out.

Brandon was left standing alone when he heard the door close behind her.

24

T HEY HAD SOMETHING up their sleeves. Mrs. Chapman scurried about the kitchen getting everything prepared. The potatoes were steaming and a pie had just come out of the oven. Alice came down and pirouetted for her mum. She was nicely dressed, and her hair was particularly pretty.

"Light a candle for the table," Mrs. Chapman suggested.

"No, Mum. He'll wonder if something's up. How do I look?"

"Like an angel. I'm going to my room. Don't go to bed until you tell me how it went."

Alice kissed her mum on the cheek.

"Go! I hear the door," Alice said as Peter came in.

He shook his umbrella and hung his coat at the door and headed for the kitchen.

"Hi, Peter."

"Why are you smiling so brightly," he asked. "Is it your birthday? No, wait, it's mine. Is it?"

Peter chuckled and smiled back just as brightly.

"No celebration, just because."

"Where's Mrs. Chapman?"

"Headache. She went to bed early."

"Oh," he said and pushed his damp wavy hair back.

"Sit down."

Alice pointed to the chair he always sat in. Sensing something was amiss, Peter looked about for clues.

"Did you paint the walls?"

"Yes," Alice replied. "Just before the war."

"Oh, then it's your hair that's different. How'd you get it that way?"

Peter got up to glance closely at the tiny bows woven in Alice's plaited hair.

"Those are tiny bows tied in your hair. You notice?"

"Yes, Peter, I noticed." Alice laughed.

"How'd you do that, I wonder?"

"Just did," she said.

"Looks so pretty. That the way you always do your hair?" he asked.

"Sometimes. Are you hungry?"

Alice ladled gravy over the pot roast she'd put on Peter's plate and placed it in front of him.

With great curiosity, Peter forked a potato to examine it as though they were new inventions.

"Are these red potatoes?" he asked.

"Yes."

"How many colors do potatoes come in, I wonder?"

"Not that many," Alice replied.

"That's good. It could be hard to remember your favorite if there were."

"I was just thinking that."

"I'm hungry. I forgot to eat lunch; guess I was wondering what Fred would say to the publishers he was showing my book to."

"Don't worry," Alice reassured Peter. "Fred talks to publishers all the time. They never get past him."

"Maggie, that was my girlfriend, she must still think I'm mad at her for losing my novel on the tube. I never told her you had a carbon. Well, I've never spoken to her again period, have I?"

"I guess she'll find out when your book is published," Alice responded.

Peter again looked at Alice's hair.

"How can your fingers tie such tiny bows?

Alice wondered if her smile revealed how much she loved the poet sitting across from her who seemed to get lost wondering about tiny bows and the colors of potatoes.

By the end of their candlelight supper, Alice had a strong feeling that Peter had noticed her, and not just as

Mrs. Chapman's daughter. They seemed to look into each other's eyes more than they chatted about potatoes. Did she get it right?

* * *

Heading to Brandon's, Maggie pondered how much she'd come to enjoy her evenings at his parents' posh townhouse over the past weeks. She wondered how rich they must be to live in Kensington and have still have a place in Paris, and another one on some tropical island, along with a ski chalet in Gstaad, Switzerland. Brandon had described each and every place in vivid detail. He even suggested that one day she'd get to see them all herself. For real? Yes, Maggie's ride may have started a bit bumpy, but still, it was glittery, and there was plenty of food for those moments when her stomach wasn't doing somersaults from fears someone would walk up to her in front of a group of people and ask her what she was reading? Reading? Yes, the times were nothing as during the war, when she and Mary ate gruel or went to bed early because there was nothing to eat.

It was sometime after eight when she arrived. Brandon said nothing about Maggie always being late and poured her a drink from the dry bar set up in the corner of the drawing room and took a seat next to her. Maggie looked anxious, so Brandon put his arm around her.

"How are things going?" she asked.

"You've got to stop worrying about all your 'things,' " he admonished. "Let me worry about sales. Every time we talk about it you seem to get worked up."

"I do? Well, at some point I guess I'm going to get that big advance you've talked about, right?" she asked. "Doesn't that have to do with sales?"

"Actually, it's not sales we should worry about," Brandon replied, even if not to her actual question.

"Then why are we always talking about them?" she asked.

"We're not, you are. You're on edge again this evening," Brandon said. "Truly, no need to worry. It's lack of sales that are the killers of careers. We're moving in the right direction, just keep following me and I'll take you where you to the heights that I promised."

Maggie got stuck wondering what Brandon had really said. It didn't quite add up. He reached to kiss Maggie on the mouth. She turned away.

"You've got to completely trust and depend on me. That's why I'm here."

"And, yes, you are. Here, I mean," she said.

"Have I ever let you down?" he asked.

"No. You fly me through the rain clouds, and look, I'm still dry. Well, come to think I'm feeling a bit damp this evening."

Brandon reached again to kiss Maggie. She didn't resist; after all, it was part of the ride she was on. Still there were moments when she wondered but they soon enough faded away. No matter how things were, they were sure as hell better than before so Maggie just held on. On to Brandon.

* * *

Alice was excited and couldn't wait to tell her mum. Peter had finally suggested they go out for supper as she and her mum had shared so many with him. She was dancing around the room with the news when Mrs. Chapman came into the kitchen.

"Dear, why are you so excited? You look as though you want to jump up and down or maybe through the window. Did I burn another hole in your blouse? I shouldn't iron while listening to the radio. It always makes me dance around the room and then I forget things."

"No, Mum. Peter has asked me out for dinner," Alice announced gleefully.

"Oh, that is good news. When's your date?"

"Saturday night. Don't burn a hole in my new pink blouse!"

"I'll turn off the radio whenever I see pink."

25

THEIRS WAS FROM the start a conflicted journey, Maggie and Peter's. But Peter had come to realize, and wondered why it had taken him so long; that he was simply boring, and it seemed as though everything that wasn't boring about him ended up on the pages of his novel. He worked at the library, where he kept his drab shirt buttoned up tight, and never did or saw much of anything. Certainly not as strange and utterly unpredictable as the woman who spent hours looking at pictures of movie stars. But once you have your life in order, and it seems to work well enough, it's not that easy to make changes. How many times did he ponder whether to change the side he parted his hair on? Well, likewise, it was surely no easier for Maggie to change and embrace conventionality. *Was that why she dumped me?* he wondered. Not because she lost his novel manuscript, but really because she thought he was boring as hell? Still in the end it's hard to change one's ways. Yet what if one could somehow find a way?

Peter's evening with Alice came and Peter spent longer than usual at the mirror near his door. He flipped his hair over to the other side, wondering if maybe he'd look more like a movie star as Maggie and her mum had suggested. But Peter only saw Peter with mussed hair. There was no glowing face or eyes with inch-long eyelashes staring back at him. Maybe he needed a change. Perhaps even splash out for another shirt— one on sale, of course. It wasn't easy being boring, but then it might be a hell of a lot harder not to be. *Certainly more costly*, he thought. Yes, being boring was like walking through life with shackles and no one notices you and no one cares should they. Not like they do movie stars anyway. Those creatures who come up with fashions the likes of which nobody'd ever seen worn before.

Peter met Alice outside the restaurant as he'd spent the day shopping for a new shirt. A whole day for one shirt? He came up against a conundrum when every shirt he reached for was nearly exactly like the one he always wore. Yep, the only ones he liked looked exactly like his drab gray shirt that no movie star would get caught dead wearing. Shopping, it would seem, was likely something movie stars didn't do for themselves. Surely, they had specially trained people, like those who polished their faces before photo-shoots, do it for them.

Alice was excited to see Peter. She noticed his new shirt and thought it was a good sign; he'd dressed up for her. She jumped up and kissed him on the cheek. Peter thought it strange. *Why would she do that?* he wondered. He'd seen her earlier in the day, and the day before, and the day before that and not one peck.

"Someone who came into the agency told me this was a really good curry place," Alice said.

"I hope it's not too hot. Is curry hot?" Peter asked.

"What happened to your hair?" Alice wondered. "Looks like you combed it one way, and then the other, and it simply capitulated near the middle."

Alice smiled and touched Peter on the cheek.

"Do you think I put too much pomade on it? I bought some this morning. The directions read use 'generously.' How much is that, I wonder?"

And he really did wonder about such things. In fact, it's the kind of thing he consulted with the man in the mirror over routinely.

Alice smiled at Peter's attempt to be glamorous. She seemed to know her way around the eatery, despite claiming it was her first time. Or perhaps it was Peter, who thought dining out was only a fish-and-chips stand, who seemed to get lost as he followed Alice following the waiter to a table in the near dark. *This dark, how would he be able to read the menu*, he wondered? *And isn't curry hot?*

"Alice, please order for us. Order anything you wish. I'm treating for introducing me to your boss, Fred." What? Then Peter had asked Alice out only as a thanks? The thought sunk deep in Alice's notion of their special dinner.

As Peter glanced over the menu, his thoughts were skidding all over, but unfortunately heading farther away from Alice's candlelit moment.

"I've been worried what Fred might say about my novel. Maybe he's changed his mind and doesn't like it."

" He loves it, Peter. He's submitting it to different publishers. That's all."

As Alice perused the menu, Peter seemed to drift into a trance, but soon came out of it thinking of Maggie again.

"But if she didn't really mean to lose my novel," he blurted out of the blue, "why does she never come to the library?"

"What… ?" Alice quickly returned to the menu and the former girlfriend wasn't on it. "What kind of curry do you want?"

"Maybe she did mean to lose it. Did she? Just to get rid of me. Is that why?"

Peter looked down the front of his new shirt. Yep, it was as drab as the other one. Almost as drab as he was. But then how could anyone be as drab as Peter? At that moment, there didn't seem to be much of a chance.

Somewhere during the lull in their broken conversation, the candle in the middle of their table suddenly blew out and with it Alice's waxing hopes for she and Peter.

26

BRANDON WAS GIVING Maggie ten pounds, or so, every week, which delighted her as it was more than she made working at the cosmetics counter in a week. He kept saying it was only an allowance of sorts and that the publishers would be sending the agency a quarterly royalty payment soon. Maggie gave some of her money to Mary and used the rest to dress, well, like a movie star, even on those days when she didn't particularly feel like much of a star of anything. Yep, things were inching up on Maggie, but she yet had no idea what or where it might lead. But a guilty conscience work in mysterious ways and can easily dodge realities.

One evening, Maggie rang Ann to meet her on her day off. Ann knew what it was like to struggle after the war, so Maggie wanted to treat her to a posh luncheon. Maggie felt she could share anything with her friend without judgment or the kind of scolding that came from Mary, a woman who was reared in an period when women were either decorations wearing lacy white dresses, if you were pretty, or seldom left the kitchen, which is where you'd end up when your prettiness wore off. Maggie knew about those kitchens; she'd helped her mum clean more than a few as a child.

At the restaurant, the same posh one that Brandon routinely took her to, Maggie sipped a martinis as she waited for Ann. Men in suits, who likely worked in the City, passed her table with their usual winks and nods. But, in those fleeting moments as they walked by their rapid fire glances suggested they imagined more. Maggie knew that there would come a day when these same men would walk past her and not notice she was even there. How far away could that day be? And then what? Go out with what was left in her purse and buy a pail and some floor brushes? There were times when Maggie felt as though she was doing nothing more than counting the days as life slipped her by. It was easy for her to go wondering when her hands would start looking like Mary's? What if it was tomorrow? How much had time caught up on her when she wasn't looking? The thought gave her chills. Tomorrows always come one day no matter how hard one pushes them back.

Ann arrived in her best suit to fit in with the surroundings. Still, she was unnerved by the glittering room.

"I can't believe you invited me to a place like this."

"Why?" Maggie asked.

The waiter appeared with menus that looked to have more pages than a telephone book.

"I didn't think they were going to let me in!" Ann announced.

"Oh, they'd look down their nose at the Queen," Maggie said. "We'll show them all!"

"We will? How?"

"We'll order everything on the menu and then eat it all then go and order more! Hey?"

They laughed. Ann loved the way Maggie could disarm a tight moment, even if she'd walked herself into it in the first place.

The waiter brought Ann a martini.

"You got enough to pay for this?" Ann whispered as soon as the man walked away. "I don't get paid till Friday."

"I have an expense account like the big boys," Maggie said with a smirk, and took another gulp of her martini.

"You most certainly… DO NOT!" Ann yelped.

They laughed. It was like old times at Selfridges where they loved to mimic Bulldog Livingston for a chuckle.

"Well, sort of do," Maggie added. "Anyway, who cares? Brandon has a house account. They'll send him the bill."

"Or send us to the back to wash dishes," Ann replied.

"Hey, we only live once, and I'm already overdrawn. How about you?"

"I never had a thing to draw on!" Ann replied.

Maggie suddenly seemed to get serious. Her eyes gazed off to one of those distant rooms where the mysteries, along with the questions, are stashed under dust covers to await the season of reckonings. One that, in Maggie's mind, was unlikely to ever come her way. No, Maggie hadn't been sleeping well for days. Her nightmares were now shaking the walls too loudly.

"Mags, what's the matter? Behind all that makeup is a sad face looking off to someplace scary."

"Scary?" Maggie chuckled and then waved her glass to the passing waiter for another round. She stretched across the table to whisper, despite the din of the crowded room.

"Annie, I'm scared," Maggie confessed.

Maggie's eyes said it all. She was scared shitless. The waiter soon appeared with second rounds.

"Keep 'em coming!" Maggie said as though she'd been assigned the starring role to play the life of the party.

Ann waived the waiter away along with that second round.

"No, waiter, that's all, thank you."

She turned to Maggie.

"What gives?" Ann asked.

Maggie gazed over the distant horizons of her broken thoughts again. Maybe to a place she longed to disappear to.

"Mags… Where are you these days?"

"You know, Mum, she never had anything. Worked all these years to just get by and there was no man around to help her. No one period, but me. And what good am I?"

"Your mum's okay, isn't she?"

"She doesn't know," Maggie said and seemed to wince.

"Know what?" Ann asked. "What are you talking about?"

"I may be in trouble. Or sure enough I'm headed down that lane, like it or not."

"Is it this situation with the agency you're always so mum about?"

"I guess, yes, you can say that."

"Is there something else maybe?" Ann asked. Maggie was silent and looked off into the distance. "Maggie, do you miss Peter?"

The question broke the damn that was already badly cracked. Maggie nodded and tears welled up in her eyes. Again, she looked off into the distance, but Peter's smile was not out there waiting to comfort her.

"I see… I had a feeling you did," Ann said.

"Well, it's too late for that one, hey?"

The diners at the next table noticed Maggie becoming emotional. But Maggie could deal with anything. She dabbed at her tears, put on a brave face along with a plastic smile and brought her chin upright again.

"Mum has always lived her dreams through me. I know she has. It would kill her if she knew."

"Knew? Maggie, what's brewing?"

"Annie, let's say, I'm way over my head and then some."

"So, bailout before anyone catches on," Ann replied. "I've done it a few times here myself. We all have."

"I think the train has left that station," Maggie said. "The only thing I can do is ride it to the edge of the cliff and then hope to jump off before it's all too late." Maggie tried to laugh. "But that only happen in the movies, doesn't it?"

"What can I do?" Ann asked plaintively.

"Don't ask any questions. I can't answer them anyway."

"You have me truly scared!"

Maggie laughed loudly to keep from crying. It caught the attention of other guests. Maggie being Maggie, simply raised her glass for a toast.

"Cheers, everyone! The war's over!"

Ann pushed Maggie's plate towards her.

"Try to eat something. Too much gin on an empty stomach isn't good news."

"How long does it take one to starve to death? What am I saying? How much time do I have?"

Maggie gulped her drink and pushed her plate back again. She reached into her purse and pulled out a pair of dark glasses she put on. They hid her from the world she could not face that day.

27

Dinner with Peter at the curry place the week before had not gone well as Peter had brought Maggie along, at least in spirit. Alice could feel her presence in Peter's every word and sigh. No matter what had happened between them, he seemed to always be looking for Maggie to return to him. But that was soon to change.

The next night, Alice had left a note under Peter's door. Fred needed to see him at the agency as soon as possible. The next day, he took off from the library during his lunch break and headed there.

Peter took a seat across from Fred and felt to see if his top button was, well, buttoned. It was as buttoned up as he was. Fred was animated and appeared to be worked up. Peter sat and listened.

"These damned publishers!" Fred said. "They drive me crazy at times."

"They don't like my novel?" Peter asked.

"Well, they have issues or maybe they're just stalling on the deal. But we can fix them. If they don't come around soon, I'll take the novel to other houses. And I will, too!"

"What don't they like?" Peter asked.

"Don't worry. I'm going to call their bluff," Fred said. "I think they may just want to get the book cheap. But I know it will be a big seller and I want you to be rewarded for all your talent and hard work."

Peter nodded. What could he say? Well, it crossed his mind again. He knew he was a boring man so like how could he possibly write anything that wasn't just as boring as he was? Peter set off with his heart dragging from behind his battered soul.

* * *

That Thursday, Ann had invited Maggie over for dinner. Only twenty minutes away on the tube, Ann's was a simple place. It had a small, makeshift kitchen that Ann had turned into a wonder, with bits and bobs hanging on every imaginable hook and device.

She reached for a skillet hanging over the two-burner stove and broke eggs for their omelet as Maggie sliced the mushrooms.

"He…"

Maggie got stuck on that single word. She shook her head to signal she didn't want to go any further with the thoughts that brewed.

"Yeah? He, who? Brandon?"

Maggie took a big gulp of her wine.

"Brandon keeps telling me he loves me, Annie."

"And you sound like that's bad news." Ann remarked.

"He wants me to marry him. He asked me last week. Actually, got on his knees like a knight-in-shining armor."

"Oh, my god!" Ann exclaimed. "He's one of the most successful agents around. Isn't that what you said?"

"I guess. Well, he's rich—lives in a townhouse that once belonged to some earl or duke. It belongs to his folks now, but they're never around, so who cares?"

"Maggie, you've come a long way from selling lipstick to women who want to look like Soho tarts."

"Yeah, and that's how far I could skid back to!"

"But why would you? If he loves you, he'll take care of you and protect you from whatever comes up in life. I mean, isn't the way it's suppose to work? At least in fairy tales, I mean."

"I told Brandon, 'wherever we end up, my mum comes, too.'"

"And?"

"He said, sure, fine. The townhouse has four floors," Maggie said.

"Golly, Mags. I live in two rooms; maybe not *that* many. I'm afraid to go see for fear I could get lost looking for rooms that never were."

"Yeah, I can see Mum sitting snug by the fire with a big smile, sipping her tea and happily knitting one of her awful sweaters."

Maggie laughed, but then teared up.

"Maggie! You're just getting married. It's been done before. The nerves will settle down. I think… I mean that's what they say."

"But all this is not like before. What am I saying? It's not like anything ever! Not for Mum. Who would have told us that we'd live in a townhouse in Kensington come one day? Yeah, like cleaning the kitchen floors maybe, but not living there like a pair of countesses, hey?"

"Golly, Mags, maybe you should take a step back to wait and see."

"Can't. I'm already hearing wedding bells ringing in my ears. That possible?"

Maggie gulped the rest of her wine waiting for the answer but Ann had already given it to her.

* * *

Alice reminded herself of what Fred had once told her; there's always a host of things brewing for publishers to consider before they decide to take offer a deal on a new book. She wasn't worried about Peter's novel. It was simply too incredible to get lost in the publishers' piles. But how could she have known of the horrific storm brewing? She was about to find out.

It was when Alice went for sandwiches that she paused in front of the bookstore she frequented on her lunch breaks. There was a large group gathered inside for a book reading. There were clearly not enough seats for everyone as many seemed to be left hanging at the aisles. There they waited impatiently to get a glimpse of this new author they'd read so much about. Maggie's poster was in the window, and didn't Olivia Holiday just look like a movie star? Brandon had sure thought so. Well, actually he'd made sure she did with a few extra pounds pushed her way.

At about that moment, a huge black sedan pulled curbside and there she was! Out came Maggie along with Ann in tow. Maggie smiled and nodded and smiled again to those waiting outside the door to get seats.

As soon as Maggie entered the bookstore, there was applause from her readers, most of whom were clutching copies of her book.

Maggie worked her way to the platform the bookstore had set up for the reading. They wanted everyone to be able to see this new author as celebrated as any movie star. She took the platform and Ann followed. Maggie did as Brandon had trained her; she nodded and smiled, and then smiled even more just in case they'd not caught the first round as they snapped her picture.

"Hi, I'm Olivia Holiday."

She sure as hell was! Well, actually she wasn't, was she? Still, her image was on the backs of all those books people were buying and the applause came in waves.

"And you know, I'm so forgetful," Maggie announced and gave another big smile to her readers. "You see, I forgot my reading glasses. So, my assistant, Ann, will have to read today. But you're in good hands as Ann is a better reader."

Well, wasn't that the truth? Maggie had finally caught Ann up on her escapades of being a writer who couldn't write. Finally, it all made sense to Ann as to what had long been going on, from Maggie's first day at Selfridges when she ask Ann to write up her sales. Maggie handed a copy of her best-selling book to Ann. She glanced at the audience, and began to read.

"It was summertime," Ann read in a soft, sultry voice. "There had been no rain all season, and his neck tasted of salt when she kissed it…"

From the back of the room, Alice watched and listened. "For all the days afterwards," Ann continued, "she promised to kiss his lips every time he looked at her, and he couldn't stop looking at her…"

"For all the days afterwards…." Alice whispered to herself. "Haven't I heard those words before?"

Could she even believe her eyes let alone her ears? At the front of the bookstore, Alice grabbed a copy of this eerily familiar book with the image of a movie star-like author and went to the cash register. As she waited to pay, her mouth gaped open thumbing through the pages.

Alice couldn't get back to the office fast enough. She even forgot to stop at the sandwich stand as her thoughts were jumbled every which way. Had Peter borrowed his words from this Olivia Holiday? Had she spent weeks typing up a manuscript that had been plagiarized? Some of it? All of it? What could the penalties for that be? Could she be implicated? But then again, this couldn't be Peter's doing, she reasoned. He was too good. So, what was going on?

Back at the office, Alice showed Olivia Holiday's book to Fred. He read a few sentences, turned a few pages, and read a few more and then flipped the book over to see the picture on the back. The one of Olivia Holiday.

"Strange. I've never heard of this author," he said.

"Well, she had a room full of people who sure have," Alice remarked.

"If the publisher finds out about this, and they're going to if they haven't already, they'll go running. In fact, perhaps that's why they've been so hard to deal with. They're buying time to sort this out."

"What do you mean?" Alice asked.

"They just may be contemplating backing out of any publishing offers they were about to put on the table. The threat of litigation for plagiarism would be expensive to defend against."

But Alice had collected her thoughts by then. It was Peter's novel, as at times, she'd seen him sitting at the breakfast table Sunday mornings, feverishly writing his pages, which he then handed to her for typing. How could he then be copying from another source?

"Peter didn't steal the words," she said.

"No, of course not, but we don't know who did," Fred said.

Alice jabbed at the picture of Olivia Holiday on the back of the novel.

"This woman! Olivia Holiday. So, what should we do?" Alice asked.

"Don't say a word for now. I've got to figure the ramifications of things before we do anything. A lawsuit would put me out of business."

"Sure, Fred. I won't say a word for now."

"I don't see any good news in this for Peter, no matter what the outcome," Fred said. "No, the book, her book for now, is already out there. The public may not ultimately care who really wrote it when they pull out their purses to buy."

28

MARY ALWAYS LOOKED forward to going to Louisa's three times a week. As of late, she couldn't think of anything she looked forward to more.

At Louisa's posh home, she'd chat, have a scone, prepare them lunch, and have a gin while Louisa washed up before they resumed their ongoing battle over who was truly the worst knitter in the Kingdom.

That afternoon, Louisa wandered out into her garden, where her roses were blooming profusely. Mary brought out a tray of cucumber sandwiches and a couple of Dubonnets over with a wedge of Meyer lemon. They headed over to the shade for refreshment.

"Which color of roses do you want to take home today?" Louisa asked.

"I still have the pink ones from Wednesday," Mary replied, and bent over to smell the tea roses.

"I'll send you home with a bunch of these yellow ones. They always make me feel so bright and sunny."

"But my dear, you're always bright and sunny," Mary quipped. "Where could I spend my afternoons and it be so delightful as when I'm here with you in your beautiful and well tended garden?"

"Yes, it is nice. Harold took great pride in the garden. You know, I do miss him at times, particularly when I'm here among his roses," Louisa said. "I mean, he had his faults, but…"

"But… he left you with piles of money to ease the pain of all

those years he struggled those long hours to make you a rich widow!"
Mary said.

They laughed and went back to their Dubonnets.

"Well, you know I never truly thought he was working during all those hours as you put it." Louisa announced. "I mean, there were more than a few times when he'd come home late with a smudge of lipstick."

Mary only smiled and lifted her glass.

"Here's to lipstick!" Mary toasted. "And now you know why I'm so glad I never had a husband!"

"You never wanted a husband? But didn't they all say we weren't worth much without one!"

"Maybe that's why? Nope, never, even for a day did I want a husband." Mary replied. "Well, maybe only for a day… or two! Long and far ago! I mean someone has to do the heavy lifting, hey?"

* * *

Alice left the agency that Friday and brought the novel by

Olivia Holiday back home with her. Fred had decided that it would be best to see what Peter thought of this author and wanted to speak to him in his office the following Monday, so Alice's discovery was soon to broadside Peter. Fred wanted her to be the first to break the bitter news.

Alice placed the book on the kitchen table with Olivia Holiday's image facing up. It would be staring up at Peter when he walked in. She'd just starting peeling the carrots that

Mrs. Chapman had washed and waiting on the counter when Peter came home. Alice didn't greet Peter as he entered, but only gestured to the book she'd placed on the table. Peter froze at what he saw. He looked stunned when he saw Maggie's picture starring up at him. He grabbed the book.

"That was my girlfriend," he said, and fell into the chair.

"You know her?" Alice asked. "Is that Maggie you're always going on about?"

"Guess her name isn't really Maggie, is it?"

Peter reached for the book and opened it. Alice watched closely as he thumbed through the pages. Peter's expressive eyes belied his grief at what was unfolding.

"But this is my novel," he said. "I don't understand. She said she lost it on the tube."

'That's what you told me, Peter," Alice replied. "Fred is looking into it. Try not to worry for now."

"It hardly looks lost here in my hand!"

"Her hand, you mean, Peter," Alice added.

Peter stared at the image of Maggie shaking his head. Suddenly it was all too clear as to why she'd disappeared from his life. It wasn't, after all, because he was the most boring man she'd ever met. Yep, Maggie had another agenda and it was far more than just living in Chelsea or driving a flashy car at Peter's side.

* * *

Maggie's strategy was to hang on tight and run faster than any mob that followed. But fear and desperation had set in big time. Whatever came up, she kept reminding herself, she'd get around it. But was she really convinced of this? No. She knew better. She knew that soon the events she was running from could become catastrophic and that she was way out of the league to manage them merely by plugging her nose. *That's why they built prisons…* she heard whispered in her tangled thoughts. Yes, the ax man was gaining, albeit very slowly at first.

Still, the weeks went by fast, what with book signings, receptions, party hopping with Brandon, and shopping for clothes at the stores he had house accounts. Maggie had much on her plate, even as she was too rattled most days to eat much of anything.

One afternoon, when most are working away at their jobs, Maggie returned from shopping and laid her fancy clothes all over the sofa. She'd picked out some pretty things for Mary, as her mum had refused to go out and shop like a rich woman.

"All for you, mum. All for you!"

"Maggie, where's the money coming from? Every time I ask, I get the runaround."

"Book's doing well," Maggie let slip nonchalantly as she wound a lovely scarf around Mary's neck, hoping it would distract her from any questions about money. But it didn't. Mary stood there looking at her daughter as if she was waiting for a confession, and there'd be grief to pay if she didn't come up with one.

"What book?" Mary demanded. "I've never seen you with a book in your hand!"

"No… ?" was all she could come up with and went about displaying her purchases. It didn't work. Mary yanked the scarf off and tossed it to the floor.

"Oh, never mind, Mum. I didn't mean it."

"What?" Mary screeched. "Didn't mean what?"

Mary grabbed the clothes spread over the sofa and tossed them into a pile on the floor.

"What book, I said? And these things are all going back. You hear me? No, I don't think you hear a thing these days!"

Mary had had enough and was mad.

Maggie also became upset. Most days, she already felt her back to the wall, and here was her own mum, banging her head against it, too.

"Mum, you're going to find out someday anyway," Maggie's eyes pleaded.

"Find out what?" Mary demanded. "Are you in some kind of trouble? Who really bought all these things?"

Maggie could yell just as loud.

"I did! I did!" she yelled. "I got a ten-pound advance. So there!"

Mary slapped Maggie's face for yelling in hers. Maggie swallowed hard, and then went back to whispering.

"I wrote a book, Mum. It's selling all over the country!"

"What in the world are you jabbering about? You didn't write nothing!" Mary howled. "You can't write the day of the week on a gro-cery list."

Tears poured down Maggie's face as she picked up the garments Mary had tossed aside and carefully refolded them. Then she angrily grabbed the pile and slung it in Mary's face.

"Oh, so what?" Maggie screamed. "Do you hear me, Mum? So what? You want me to return these to the stores? Then, you come and show me how it's done and then along the way we can talk about all the years we wore rags."

Maggie grabbed her mum's frayed sleeve where there was a worn hole, to make her point.

Mary lifted her hand as if she were about to smack Maggie again. Maggie put her face into Mary's to take the strike. But Mary started to cry and her raised hand went limp.

"Oh, god, you're in real trouble." Mary said. "I can tell! I should have known!"

"No, but I'm headed there, and you're coming along for the ride. You see, I'm getting married, Mum. Married!"

Mary could only collapse on the sofa.

"Well, that shut you up!" Maggie said.

Maggie fell on the sofa next to her mum and put her head on her mum's lap, as she'd done since she was a child.

"I don't know what else to do," Maggie confessed through tears. "I'll take these things back if it will make you happy, but it's not going to make any difference. It's all way past due now!"

Yes, Maggie was up against the wall, and there was no room to back up or out. Anyway, it wouldn't delay the cataclysm that was coming. That hope was gone. Maybe the only thing she could do was buy time, close her eyes, and hope for a good spot to leap off before the situation swallowed her alive.

"What do you mean, Mags?"

"Mum, I have to marry Brandon. Who else can save me now?"

"You see, I knew you were in trouble. And now it sounds like you're digging yourself in deeper. You're going off to marrying a man I've never met and I don't think you even know him yourself. Is he the one buying all these clothes?"

"You were right, Mum. You always are. I've been digging my grave for months now."

"No! You can fix things. Whatever you've dug yourself into, go and dig yourself back out before it's too late," Mary pleaded.

"Mum, I think it's too late. If I don't come up with something soon, I know they're gonna come for me."

"Who?" Mary pleaded. "Who's coming for you?"

"I don't know. Don't know. Who cares anyway?"

"I do!" Mary pleaded.

"I know, Mum. We've always been there for each other and that's because no one else was. So, maybe things will be better with Brandon."

"And what if he's not? There for you?" Mary asked and wiped her last tear.

"Then I'm dead, and then what about you? What happens to women who have no job, and no husband? Hey? Want to go take a long walk around SoHo to see?

29

S PREAD OUT OVER the imported carpet in Brandon's posh drawing room, Maggie and Ann ate crackers and cheese as they poured over magazines with pictures of weddings. Maggie poured them a glass of wine as Ann put a record on the phonograph.

"Where'd you say Brandon was?" Ann asked.

"He's visiting his parents in Paris. How is it?"

"This wine tastes like it probably cost ten pounds," Ann remarked.

"You can taste the price tag? They all taste the same to me. Brandon has a wine cellar in the basement."

"Of course, he does. Doesn't everyone have a wine cellar?" Ann asked. "Mine's in a box under my bed. I have so many bottles, I should really install a light under there so I can count them."

"Cheers! To the posh life," Maggie said and raised her glass. "Brandon still wants the wedding in Paris. I guess because that's where his parents spend most of their time."

"Paris? But you're an English girl," Ann said.

"Mum said the same. Told me she'd never cross the Channel for nobody and that definitely includes 'nobody' me these days."

"Where will you live?" Ann asked. "Surely not Paris, hey?"

"Why not here? His folks are never around," Maggie replied. "Brandon said they can't wait to meet me and may come over before the wedding just to get to know their future daughter-in-law."

"Ah, yes. It's always tough getting started," Ann remarked. "Money's tight, only a stack or two laying about, and there's only so many bottles in the wine cellar to drink. On top of it, you end up living in your in-law's place in the heart of Kensington not even five blocks from the palace."

They laughed as they looked about the posh room.

"What about your book tour?" Ann asked.

"I can't sleep, I'm so scared!" Maggie said. "I've tried, but Brandon says there's no way out of it."

"You're going to have to read, you know? " Ann reminded Maggie. "And then what?"

"That's why you're coming. You've got to. I don't want any person on earth seeing me wear glasses."

They laughed.

"Here's to books by the thousands," Ann toasted.

"I'm going down for another bottle. Here, put the cork back in the bottle. Brandon will never notice we've had one, or two on him!"

Ann shoved the cork back into the empty bottle and handed it to Maggie.

"Bring two bottles in case there's a shortage coming on," Ann said.

* * *

Fred had been busy on Peter's behalf. He felt certain there'd likely been a crime committed, and Peter was surely the victim. Fred had turned the matter over to the

Crown Prosecutor's office.

It was a dark and rainy day when Crown Prosecutor Bingley showed up at Fred's office to discuss the book that was selling by the boatloads and was eerily the same as Peter's manuscript. Peter arrived shortly after the prosecutor. Alice showed him into Fred's office, where they'd been going over things.

"Peter, take a seat. This is Prosecutor Bingley. We've been discussing your book and he wants to ask you a few questions."

"Yes, Sir," Peter replied. "I'm here for that."

Peter seemed uneasy. The prosecutor noticed his hands fidgeting in his lap.

"You also, Alice," Fred said. "As you're the one who uncovered this issue."

Prosecutor Bingley pulled out a copy of the novel and began his questions.

"Peter, as you know, this book by Olivia Holiday…" he said.

"Purportedly to be by Miss Holiday," Fred interjected.

"Yes, that is the issue, isn't it? Who wrote the book that has now sold sizable numbers and has surely filled someone's pockets with a great deal of money," Bingley said.

"Maggie, or Olivia Holiday, was my girlfriend," Peter said looking down at his feet.

"Best just to answer the prosecutor's questions," Fred suggested.

"Did you contribute to the writing of the novel that I have in my hand?" Bingley asked.

"No, Sir," Peter announced.

"What? No, you say?" Fred asked incredulously.

"What he means is, he wrote it," Alice said. "All of it, and no one contributed to it. I know because I typed it from his handwritten manuscript. In fact, I typed it twice—the second time after Peter's manuscript was lost by Maggie, or Miss Holiday, or whatever her real name is."

"Then I presume you have the original handwritten manuscript?" Bingley asked Peter. "Yes?"

"No. I threw it out," Peter said.

"Peter, do you understand the implications of this?" Prosecutor Bingley asked.

"Yes, Maggie was not my real girlfriend."

"If Miss Holiday can prove that she wrote the novel, in part by producing her rough drafts, then I fail to see how you might have a case. You can't go accusing someone of being a plagiarist without something to back it."

"Yes, I know," Peter said so quietly he could barely be heard.

"But if you are the true author of this work, as Fred and Alice insist, then Miss Holiday is a plagiarist and has committed a serious crime of fraud to enrich herself," Bingley stated.

"But she didn't mean to do it," Peter responded.

"No? She didn't mean to steal your novel, have it published in her own name, and keep all the money?" Bingley asked.

"I guess she just wanted to live like a movie star," Peter added.

"So do bank robbers," Bingley quipped.

"Yeah, apparently she is," Fred added. "I mean living high these days."

"And you're paying for it, Peter," Alice remarked.

At that, Peter was reminded that he was always worried about having enough put back to make his bi-weekly payment on his electric hotplate.

"I have enough information to ask Miss Holiday a few questions."

At that, Bingley got up to leave.

In the outer office, Alice stopped him.

"Sir, Peter told me something I think you should know about this Miss Holiday."

"Yes?"

Alice approached and whispered.

"I see. That is interesting. Very interesting, indeed. Thank you, Miss."

Prosecutor Bingley smiled and opened his umbrella to leave.

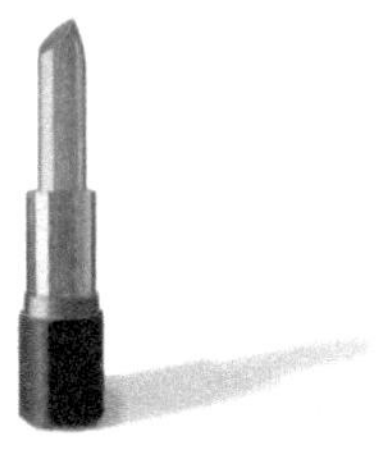

30

MARY WAS PLAYING cards at the neighbors' when Ann arrived for supper with Maggie. Mary had left a kettle of soup on the stove, along with a loaf of bread she'd picked up that morning. As they ate their soup, Maggie and Ann caught up on things.

"Brandon still wants to get married in the fall," Maggie said. "He says it's the most romantic time of the year. I don't know if I want to wait that long."

"Why are you in such a rush now?" Ann asked. "Last month you wondered if you should jump off like Brandon was a burning building.

Maggie dropped her spoon in her soup and pushed the bowl away.

"Annie, I don't love Brandon. I know he loves me, he never stops telling me so, and I know he'll take care of me and Mum; still, I just don't have that kind of feeling for him."

"You can't and go and marry someone just so they'll take care of you," Ann said.

"You don't know how hard it's been for us, me and Mum. She's not been well lately, and I think it's because of all the grief I've caused her. I'm afraid I'll end up breaking her heart."

"I don't understand," Ann replied. "What's not going well now?"

"Things are going well enough, I guess," Maggie replied. "But what about next month, and the year after that?"

Maggie pulled her bowl of soup back.

"Whatever, hey? I don't know if I could ever love anyone again, so why not have a go with Brandon? I could get used to living in a town-house with a wine cellar and a big black car taking me around. Anyway, when does love ever last? Didn't for Mum and look where that left her!"

Maggie took a deep breath. One of resolution.

* * *

The following week, Prosecutor Bingley showed up at Brandon's office without an appointment. He was working at his desk when Sandra entered to announce him.

"Sir, I have the Crown Prosecutor here."

Sandra motioned for Bingley to take a seat across from Brandon's desk.

"I can't imagine what this visit could be about?" Brandon said nonchalantly.

"No? Just a few questions. Fairly routine."

"Sandra, close the door."

Brandon smiled, but it was obvious he wasn't comfortable with the unexpected visit; after all, prosecutors don't show up unexpectedly. No, they tend to like to snoop without anyone doing any house cleaning beforehand.

Prosecutor Bingley pulled out of his attaché a tablet and perused his notes flipping from one page to the next.

"Sir, you've been a literary agent for how long? I think I have it down here somewhere."

Brandon was strangely uneasy with this question. "Oh, nearly ten years," Brandon replied cautiously.

"Have you ever faced any legal issues with any of your clients?"

"No, never," he said. "I'm known to be an excellent judge of talent. I represent some of the most brilliant writers in the U.K."

"That's what I understand. Your client, Miss Holiday, is your client, isn't she?"

"Yes, she is, and my fiancée."

"Congratulations, I'm sure."

"What is the purpose of this visit?" Brandon asked.

"When a book is as successful as Miss Holiday's, there's bound to be issues that come up. Happens all the time," Prosecutor Bingley stated.

"Issues? What kind of issues?" Brandon demanded and squirmed in his seat like it was getting a bit toasty for him.

"I'll get to that, but for now, I wonder if you could arrange for me to ask your client a few questions. Here in your office would be fine."

"Yes, of course," Brandon replied. "Next week, at your convenience."

At that, Brandon definitely felt like he was on the hot seat and what made it worse, he was clueless as to why. But clearly something had to be up.

* * *

That evening, a very uptight Brandon had Maggie over for supper. He wondered what was up and what she knew and, most of all, if it could fall on his head. He was simmering the sauce for the pasta when things also got heated between them.

"I pulled a bottle out of the rack in the cellar. It was empty," he said, rather annoyed that his wine cellar had been pilfered. Brandon had long embraced a philosophy that what was his, was his, and what was yours was his also, if he fancied it. This was a one way street he traveled.

"Rats probably got to it," Maggie replied. "Must'a had a great party once they got that cork out!"

Brandon didn't find this amusing. He stood there simmering hotter than his sauce.

"I thought you loved my delicious humor," she said before reaching over to turn the heat under the saucepan to full throttle. The flames enveloping the pan also seemed to scorch Brandon's mood. He jumped to turn it down again.

"A little charcoal in the spaghetti sauce is good for you!" she said with a grin.

"I don't like this?"

"Rats having a party on your coin?"

"Why is the prosecutor wanting to talk to you? In my office?"

"Why don't you ask him?"

"Don't be cheeky. These guys don't come around to chat about the weather," he announced.

"That's good news, given it's rained for ten days straight."

Maggie was in no mind to confess. After all, Brandon's pasta sauces weren't that good.

Still, Maggie had already been wondering when the good times would be over—no more shopping, and she'd surely be making notches on a cell block wall to mark the day she'd be getting out. But then again, what if they forgot about her and never let her out? Things happen you know, and some folks are never heard from again. These thoughts kept bouncing back no matter how hard or far Maggie slung them aside.

"What are we going to do?" Maggie asked.

"We, is it?And do about what?"

"What do you mean?" Maggie asked. "You always told me you would protect me."

"From?" Brandon interrupted. "From what, Maggie? From yourself? Something's up and it obviously has nothing to do with me, does it?"

"Oh, it's me, is it?" Maggie howled in Brandon's face. "You're the one that's been leading me down the nod and smile path all these months."

Maggie gulped her wine. But on the last swallow, her thoughts went deaf when she suddenly realized there were no wedding bells drumming in her ears. In fact, she was all but certain the only thing she could hear was the executioner sharpening his ax. But it was only her teeth grinding from anger.

31

MARY WAS DEEPLY worried about the situation Maggie had gotten herself into, in part because she simply didn't know what was going on. But then neither did Maggie, at least not to the degree she'd dug herself in. In Maggie's mind, she was merely on joy ride that might make her life and that of her mum, a bit easier. In the end, what could go wrong on the path to a 'somewhere better'?

To calm her nerves, Mary's therapy was always to work hard on her knitting. She sat there knitting as fast as her needles would twist, turn, and knot. And those knots were only getting tighter. Yep, as tight as a hangman's noose. Maggie noticed her mum's anxiety and broke the heavy silence between them.

"Mum, I think it's time for a holiday. Wouldn't that be nice?"

Mary didn't look up. She simply sped up her needles to convey what she thought of Maggie's notion.

"Huh? What are you jabbering about now?"

"Sure, why not?" Maggie asked.

"Holiday? You gonna reschedule Christmas?" Mary asked. "Only the King can do that!"

"We should get away," Maggie announced. "Go over to the continent. I have nearly fifty pounds put back. Maybe more if I return some clothes," she said. "And I bet Brandon will buy the tickets just to get rid of me now!" Maggie added under her breath.

"Where in the world did you get that kind of money? I've never in my life had that much to my name."

"I've told you over and over again. Brandon, Mum, Brandon. For the wedding," Maggie said. "Will that do?"

"So, then why do you want to go abroad so close to your wedding? It doesn't make sense. Nothing you say or do these days makes sense."

Mary pulled back the drape to see the rain pelting the window. Then, she threw her knitting down. That signaled she was truly mad.

"You're always telling me I'm worn with worries and need a holiday. Yes?" Maggie asked.

"What are you going on about?" Mary demanded. "Every young girl gets nerves come the wedding."

"Mum, I can't answer your questions," Maggie said.

"What questions? I haven't asked you any questions!"

"I want you to pack a small bag for a long holiday. Leave it over there at the door for now," Maggie stated.

"Small bag, long holiday, hey? Now doesn't that sound interesting? And for what? It's too cold to go to the bus stop!"

"Mum, what have we been talking about?" Maggie yelled.

"We're not talking about anything!" Mary screeched back.

"I said we're going over the Channel somewhere for a stay. Sure, why not?" Maggie said.

"The continent? No, I have no idea what you're talking about," Mary said.

"I said, I can't answer your questions. Just be ready."

"Ready for what, I said?" Mary screeched again. "What?"

"Mum, I'm trying to tell you, I don't exactly know," Maggie replied. "And I don't know when we'll leave. I need to get the tickets. We'll go off and enjoy a spell in France. Yes, that will be nice for us. Maybe I can get a job over there. Sure, I can wait tables at some café. We'll get a little cozy room, and you can sit there and knit all day."

"Who goes to France in the middle of winter? To knit?" Mary demanded. "Anyway, I've never been out of England, and I never will! If

God wanted us to go to France, he'd not have put the English Channel between us."

"Then stay!" Maggie yelled. "But I'm getting out!"

"Out of what?" Mary demanded.

But Maggie had left the room in more ways than one.

* * *

Over the next few weeks, Maggie was so preoccupied with her new "office job," as she always referred to it, that she didn't notice Mary slipping out most mornings. But then Mary wasn't schlepping her bucket; she just left it at Louisa's, where it sat by the rear service door collecting dust. Mary and Louisa had determined that there were more important things to get to than mopping floors, such as a bottle of gin and two lonely glasses longing to be filled with laughter.

They sat around Louisa's breakfast table, catching up and drinking up. If Louisa didn't want Mary bothering with the dust, at least Mary felt she could teach her how to knit awful sweaters.

"I come by three times a week and do nothing but drink your gin and eat your scones," Mary said.

"Well, I wouldn't say that. After all, you've taught me how to be the worst knitter in London!" Louisa proclaimed. "That's something we can talk about. I mean, I can't take the blame myself, can I?"

"Oh, you're not so bad. You just need to go out and adopt a three-legged dog for the sweater you're still knitting," Mary said. "That's a sweater you're still calling it, dear?"

Louisa held up her sweater and counted two sleeves and still the other one she'd forgotten.

"Honestly, I'm not sure what it will be one day. Got any ideas?" Louisa declared. "Three holes. I guess I'll tell folks the moths got to it before I'd finished."

"Sounds good to me," Mary said. "Pour me another, dear."

Louisa put her knitting into her bag and poured Mary another Dubonnet. Suddenly, she became very serious.

"Mary, I've always wanted to tell you something—something that I could never quite get out, and I feel guilty about that. Truly, I do."

"Oh, my word, what is it Louisa?"

"I love you, Mary! I do."

"You do? And so, tell me why?"

"Because all those years you came 'round to clean, and Harold was here most the time after he retired, but you never made me feel guilty…"

"Guilty? Whatever for what?" Mary asked incredulously.

"For taking him away from you of course!"

Mary started laughing, took another swig of her Dubonnet, and went on laughing all the harder. That got Louisa to howl right alongside her.

"Why are you laughing? I've been burdened with that guilt for years!"

So then Louisa laughed harder than Mary and took another gulp of her drink.

"You thought you'd taken Harold away from me?" Mary asked.

"Well, didn't I?"

"No!" Mary replied. "I never loved Harold. Not for one minute. Well, maybe a few moments here and there. But I knew you did. Oh sure, he was a good looking, but nope, I never loved the man. All the same, I got exactly what I wanted from him. Yes, I did. Then I dumped him on your doorstep! Had to find a place to put him or for sure he'd never leave me be."

"Dumped him?" Louisa screeched, "On me, you say?"

"Well, Louisa, who else would have him?"

They laughed all the more.

"You dumped him on me, hey?"

"Sent him packing, Louisa. Came the day when I couldn't get rid of him fast enough."

"So, what did you want from Harold that you got all the same?"

"I'll show you."

Mary reached for her pocketbook and pulled out a photo of Maggie. With a big smile, she handed it over the table to Louisa.

"This is my Maggie. She's a grown woman now."

"Oh, my goodness. And she looks just like Harold!" Louisa said.

"I told you he was a looker!" Mary said. "And that's all I ever wanted from him."

Louisa lifted her glass for a toast.

"Here's to our Harold. May he rest in peace and all his money continue to draw interest for eternity!"

"Yes, to Harold and the beautiful daughter he gave me!"

Well, you've heard it said before; things happen! They sure enough do, don't they?

32

MAGGIE HADN'T HEARD from Brandon for days. That was surely confirmation, she thought, that he would throw her under the bus if it came to it. Yep, smile, nod, and run. But then he rang her, or actually Sandra did, requesting she drop by his office that Wednesday at one o'clock sharp. *Why?* Maggie wondered. *And why had Sandra called and not Brandon?* Her instincts told her the time had come! Time to flee before the last boat left for Calais. But she showed up anyway. With lingering thoughts that maybe she could still ride the train a bit longer, or at least hold on until she could convince Mary they'd love living in France. Yeah, right!

Prosecutor Bingley was seated across from Brandon when Maggie appeared. She was wearing a traveling suit. She'd left her bag near the door at the flat, and had packed Mary's as her mum knitted away, ignoring her daughter's chattering about some misguided adventure across the Channel.

"Olivia, this is Crown Prosecutor Bingley. He'd like to ask you a few questions." Brandon was not smiling. Maggie wondered what they'd been talking about? She eased herself into the seat, figuring it could only be bad news and glanced again at the door to gauge how close it was should she need to skip over to the docks rather hurriedly.

"Yes, of course. But I do have an engagement soon. My mum and I are going off for some shopping."

She was disinclined to say the spree was to be in Paris.

"Miss Holiday, you're a very successful writer. You've sold a lot of books. Did you go to university?" the prosecutor asked.

Maggie was stymied. Yep, with those very words, her heart could feel the train take on speed as it headed for the cliffs of Dover! About then it seemed as though the velocity of events had caused her mouth to shut down as nothing came out at first. She sat there and squirmed as if the question, like the rain that day, would simply go away if she ignored it long enough. It didn't, they didn't. No, the prosecutor sat waiting for an answer and his eyes never left hers as he did.

"Miss Holiday is a natural talent," Brandon piped in and looked to Maggie for support of his rendition of the truth. "Some of my most successful writers never finished university." Again he looked at Maggie but she only smiled and nodded at him in retaliation for his smugness.

But the prosecutor had a sixth sense for malarkey and wanted a real answer.

"Did you not finish university, Miss Holiday?"

"No, Sir," Maggie replied.

"She was busy writing big novels," Brandon added.

"Yes, of course. How many novels have you written? Bingley asked.

"She's working on her third," Brandon said. "Isn't that right, Olivia?"

Maggie decided the moment called for her to utilize what Brandon had long taught her; simply nod and smile, and all would be good. Well, maybe not this time. It suddenly started to look as though Brandon had gotten his theory all wrong.

Still her repeated glances at the door to Brandon's office made her appear to be planning an escape. Bingley noticed and wondered why such a successful writer would have difficulty responding to simple questions. Of course, he knew, didn't he? Alice had filled him in on Maggie's secret—a tidbit that Peter had shared with her that she could not read. All this squirming about was typical of the guilty party, the prosecutor surely thought, as those who were not guilty were forthcoming, and in fact, eager to help the Crown get their man, woman, or wonton plagiarist.

"For the novel you just published, did you type it as you wrote it? Or did you write it out longhand first? Bingley wanted to know.

Maggie couldn't hear the question as her thoughts were fogged and hearing bad from the screeching train whistle signaling she was headed for doom that was likely just ahead.

She looked to Brandon for support. He looked at the prosecutor to see if he could read where the man was headed with these rather silly and certainly intrusive questions.

"Did you keep your notes and drafts, etc.?"

"Why, yes," she lied. "And I gave them all to Brandon, didn't I?"

Brandon sat back in his seat as Maggie had never given him anything but her novel manuscript, all nicely typed by Alice.

"May I see these?" Bingley asked Brandon. "Are they at hand?"

"Ah, no, they're not," Brandon stammered.

Prosecutor Bingley waited for more. Brandon squirmed in his seat again.

"You see, I don't keep rough drafts in the office. Takes up too much space. But I can pull them out of storage if you wish."

With that, Brandon almost looked as though he was being truthful. But Bingley decided he'd catch the man in his own lie and proceeded to do just that.

"Let me make a note here. Do you have a piece of paper I may use? I seem to have used mine up."

"Yes, of course."

Brandon handed the prosecutor a piece of paper. Bingley smiled and then handed it to Maggie as if it were a box of bonbons. But she looked at it as though there was a dead rat laying there staring up at her. And then the rat winked; actually, it was Brandon who winked. Well, no he hadn't, but Maggie wished he'd signaled he was somehow behind her. But nope, no deal from the heel.

"Oh, Miss Holiday, perhaps you can help me with something?"

The very words were like a jolt of lightning as Maggie could easily anticipate what the next question would be. Bingley waved that paper at her as Brandon looked on perplexed as hell. Maggie glanced over to the door again.

"Miss Holiday, just for my report, please write the first sentence of your novel."

Maggie swallowed hard and looked to Brandon, wondering if the prosecutor could hear her heart pounding. Of course, Brandon did not possess a heart. It wasn't something he could purchase on account.

"Olivia, I mean, Miss Holiday…" Brandon said, looking annoyed that Maggie appeared to be acting like a diva.

"I'd prefer not to," she said just like one.

Then, she nodded and smiled. But what could she have said? A full confession was out of the question as it would have taken too long as she was already late for her shopping trip to Paris.

"Why?" Brandon screeched at Maggie. "Just do it."

"That's okay," Bingley said. "I don't want to make

Miss Holiday feel like she's on the spot here. Is that how you feel, Miss?"

Maggie nodded and smiled thinking that just sitting there like a lump wouldn't persuade anyone of anything, but it also wouldn't convict her either. Would it? Still things can happen!

"I understand. Writing a sentence from her own book may be an imposition. That right?"

"I don't get it! Just write the damned sentence!" Brandon yelled.

"You write it!" Maggie screeched back. "You're the one always saying you'll take care of everything!"

"Take care of what things, Miss Holiday?" Prosecutor Bingley asked. "What has your agent taken care of?"

"Nothing! Can't you see that for yourself?" Maggie looked at Brandon as if she wanted to stab him in the eye with an envelope opener. Or maybe a blunt book.

At that, Bingley headed another direction.

"When can I see those early drafts of the novel? Just the first novel," he asked Brandon.

"Soon. I'll call you next week," Brandon said.

"I'll be waiting for your call."

Prosecutor Bingley gave Maggie a long look as though he expected her to start spilling her frustrations, anger, and perhaps a few morsels of the truth. But she only feigned a slight smile and a rather limp nod.

Bingley was no sooner out of the office when Brandon went over and slammed his door closed.

But Maggie had heard the message before Brandon delivered it. He pointed to the blank paper in front of Maggie.

"Write the first sentence!" he seethed.

Maggie only stared at him.

"Write any sentence! Write anything! Write!"

But Maggie shook her head no and smiled. It was only theme-and-variation of what Brandon had always told her to do. He knew it, and it made him livid.

"Oh, my god! It can't be! You can't read or write, can you?"

Maggie slung him a partial grin to make up for not coming to her rescue.

"Oh, god! I'm dead in the water! They'll take away my license!"

This time Maggie nodded in the affirmative and smiled big time!

Brandon grabbed the blank piece of paper, tore it to shreds, and tossed it in Maggie's face.

Maggie stood up, dusted off the pieces of paper, smiled, nodded again and existed Brandon's office. She could hear Brandon's screeching all the way to the street. It sounded a bit like a train wreck.

33

THE NEXT EVENING at Brandon's didn't go any better. The smiles and nods slung back and forth between Maggie and Brandon the previous day were now near to being flaming swords. In the kitchen, Maggie watched and waited for Brandon to direct traffic as he always did. He paced the room and stared at Maggie with anger.

"What are we going to do?" she asked.

"We is it? Seems like your name is on that novel," he said.

"You said you would take care of everything," Maggie reminded.

"When did I say that?" Brandon demanded.

"When I became a top-selling novelist," she screeched, and downed the rest of her wine.

"I'll tell you what. You learn how to write a fucking sentence for the Prosecutor, and I'll fix everything else!"

Maggie decided to tread water to see what might happen. Would Brandon toss her a life-preserver, or push her head under the wave she was already drowning in?

"After we're married, I'm not going to write anymore," Maggie announced so softly he could barely hear her. Still he heard loud and clear. With those few words Brandon went ballistic.

"What? What did you just mumble? Are you out of your mind?" he screamed. "You've never written anything in your pathetic life, and I'm sure as hell not going to marry you!"

"You said you loved me," she reminded him.

"What I love is money. Just like you, Maggie! That's the only thing we have in common and it takes a pile of it to live in Kensington."

"You said this place was owned by your rich parents, who live in Paris in an even bigger place! Wasn't that your story? One of your damned stories!"

"My parents are dead, you fool! And they sure as hell weren't rich. My dad was a butcher in Shropshire. The mortgage here takes up most of what I pull in. I only bought it to draw big authors to the agency. And you, it now seems, are no longer a big author!"

"What are we going to do?" she pleaded.

"Get it out of your head! There is no 'we' here. That ended when I found out there was no bestselling novelist… here!"

"You were using me all along then, weren't you?"

"And who did you use, Maggie? Have you forgotten that you didn't write the novel that has your name printed on it? Or maybe it was a printing error, like the rest of you is one big fuck up."

"You only care about the book and how much money it would make for you!"

"How's that different than you? You only care about the book you didn't write and how much money it would make for you! You're going to be in serious trouble, and I'm not going to let you take me down with you!"

Brandon wiped the sweat off his forehead.

"Find the front door and lose my number. I'm through with you!"

Maggie walked out of Brandon's place and his life. All the way home she wondered how she could tell her mum there was to be no wedding and there'd be no one on earth who could save her at this point.

* * *

Well, the day had to come around at some point. Yes, Peter's daily excursions spent wondering what had happened to Maggie had come to an end. It was now clear to him that she'd used him, and perhaps even set him up for it. He recalled when she seemed so delighted to discover that he was writing a novel, and quickly put together a posh life of the novelist—one that apparently did not include him. After all, when did she ever ask him what *his* dreams were? Not even what color sports car he wanted. Well, clearly Maggie's books were stacked somewhere else, and obviously always were. Peter now watched as Maggie strolled along on this path of hers of becoming, if not a movie star, at least a celebrity novelist. One who could not write the day of the week on a scrap of paper. Peter felt used and grew angry. He'd long blamed himself for losing Maggie thinking it was all due to how utterly boring he was. Now he was relieved she was gone from his life for good.

On Friday, Fred asked Alice if she would request Peter stop by his office the following Monday. He wanted to go over Prosecutor Bigley's final report on the Crown's case against Maggie. Fred was concerned about how to inform Peter of the news and the consequences it would ultimately have on this Olivia Holiday.

Peter arrived at the agency at noon. Alice had picked up the usual sandwiches for them, but Peter shook his head. He'd lost his appetite and had hardly slept all weekend.

"Peter, I've gone over this memo from the prosecutor's office. They plan to prosecute Olivia Holiday, Maggie, if you wish, for fraud. She could see jail time. In fact, I'm sure she will. How shall we proceed?"

"I don't understand?" Peter said.

"For Maggie to be prosecuted, you must be a witness as you and the publisher of the book with her name on it were defrauded."

"Yes, Maggie lied to me all along. She only wanted to live like a celebrity. I can see that now," Peter said. "Will I have to go to court?"

"Yes, certainly you must appear. There you'll tell the judge what happened. It's really out of our hands after that."

"Thank you."

Peter, looking morose, left Fred's office and paused at Alice's desk.

"She used me, Alice. All she ever wanted was my novel. Not me."

"I think you're right, Peter," Alice replied. "She will be punished for all the grief she's caused.

"Fred says she will go to prison."

"You're doing the right thing," Alice added.

Peter left feeling empty. His emotions where headed towards the nearest storm drain. But soon the entire story of Maggie and her dreams of being a celebrity would be over. The curtain was about to come down on Maggie's long solo performance of being an author, and so would a prison sentence.

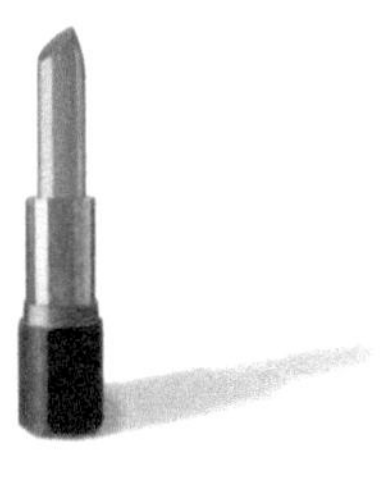

34

B RANDON HAD ABANDONED ship as soon as he figured it might soon be taking on water. He wasn't the sort to hang around for bad news. Maggie felt ashamed that she'd not seen through him, but she again came to terms with the fact she'd never loved him, although she figured, or, at least hoped, she might come to one day. But then, truth be told, she was only looking for a knight-in-shining armor to slow the train wreck headed her way; a ride of a lifetime that she'd never bought a ticket for.

Maggie figured that as now there'd be no one to come to her rescue, they'd probably be picking her up soon. She became numb with fear. Not only for having never been in jail, but for what was likely to happen to Mary when she was gone. Mary hadn't done anything wrong, she reasoned, but would pay a heavy price for Maggie's wild-eyed schemes to make their lives a better place.

She was sitting at the table pondering all the gruesome realities when they came for her. There was a loud pounding on the old door to their flat. Maggie jolted as though she expected them to knock it down. Finishing the washing up, Mary dropped one of her precious floral-painted plates she was towel drying.

"Oh, my god!" Mary exclaimed. "Who could that be at this time of night?"

Maggie sat in silence as though she'd not heard the pounding on the door. But it continued.

"Don't open it!" Mary screeched. "They're robbers!"

"No, Mum." Maggie's voice cracked. "I'm the robber. They've come for me. Go let them in! Please, Mum. Do as I say."

"What?" Mary was terrified, and even more so when the pounding became louder and louder. Mary was frozen with fear. Maggie went to open the door. She'd barely turned the knob when the door flew open and two police barged in.

"What are you doing here?" Mary screeched.

"We've come for Maggie," the policewoman informed them, and looked at Maggie. "Do you go by the name Olivia Holiday?"

"Of course, she doesn't!" Mary yelled.

"Yes, Mum. That's me," she told them.

"What are you talking about?" Mary asked. "You're no Olivia Holiday. Tell them!"

"Be still, Mum."

"You're under arrest. Please get up and come quietly with us."

"No! She's not who you're looking for!" Mary yelled and went to her cupboards for a weapon; something heavy she could throw at them or maybe a big knife.

"I wouldn't do that if I were you," the policewoman said. "We will take you in as well!"

"Where are you taking her?" Mary pleaded.

"To jail, Mum. Please sit down and try to stay calm. I'll be alright."

The policewoman handcuffed Maggie and led her away. Mary's shrieks could be heard up and down the landing outside their flat.

Hearing the commotion, Dora and Primrose were soon at Mary's door. Mary looked over the railing to the wet street below. Down there, the police put Maggie in a police car. She tried to control her sobs until she was out of her mum's view. But it didn't work. Mary felt every one.

"Where are they taking her?" Mary sobbed.

"We'll find out. But it's too late to do anything now," Primrose said as Dora eased Mary back into the flat. She had to do something. Now, Mary was beginning to see why Maggie had wanted her to pack a bag and head across the Channel.

Back in the kitchen, Mary sat at the table sobbing uncontrollably. Her packed traveling case still waiting near the door. The sight of it made her wail more. Dora tried to comfort her.

"We should have gone to France!" Mary got out.

"Right now, you've got to get in there and get some sleep in Maggie's room," Dora said. "I'll be here sleeping on your sofa."

"Yeah, we'll be right here if they call," Primrose added.

"But who will call?" Mary pleaded.

"The authorities."

"How late does the tube run?" Mary asked.

"You're not going anywhere tonight. You don't even know where they took her. You can't go out there looking. Tomorrow, right Dora?"

"Yeah, tomorrow. After you've had some sleep."

Mary took a deep and uneven breath and resigned herself that there was nothing she could do that late. But she was already figuring on what she would do the next morning.

* * *

That night Mary couldn't sleep. She tossed and turned, and when she heard Dora snoring on the sofa, she gave up and went in to make a pot of tea. But it was only a bit after four o'clock. She didn't know what time the tube started running, but she was sure it couldn't be that early.

Only a few minutes after six, with Dora still sound asleep, Mary slipped out the door and headed to the tube station. *Why are there so many people out so early?* she wondered. The train was crowded and seemed louder than most mornings, but then her nerves were all but flayed.

This time it seemed to take forever to get to Louisa's. She didn't let herself in with her key. She knocked. Moments later, Louisa opened the door.

"Is this Wednesday?" she asked Mary.

"My Maggie, she's in trouble. Don't know what to do," Mary asked. Her expression said volumes. She and Mary had chatted about Maggie so many times that Louisa felt she knew her, even though it had been years since she'd helped her mum clean at the Harolds'.

"Why'd you knock? Forget your key?" Louisa asked.

"Didn't want to frighten you if I barged in too early."

"Frighten me, you say?" Louisa said. "We survived the war, and I should be so easily frightened? Come in and sit while I make us some eggs. Then you can tell me what this is all about."

Mary couldn't say much about the situation because she didn't understand what had happened. Just that it was about a book and Maggie was a robber who'd been taken away like any criminal.

"I think I get it. Maybe, anyway," Louisa said. "You stop crying. It will only exhaust you more. I want you to take a rest in the guest room. I'll make some calls and see what I can come up with. I'll go to Harold's desk and pull out his telephone numbers. He knew nearly everyone in government. Go on now and lay down. I'll come in later and check on you."

Mary dragged herself up, kissed Louisa on the forehead, and went to lay down.

Louisa was soon in the study looking for phone numbers to call. Finally, she found one that looked like it might be promising. She got on the telephone.

"Mark, this is Louisa Harold," she said. "Yes, I know. Harold talked about you often. You know he always said you were the smartest man in Westminster. Listen, I have a friend. It seems her daughter…"

Louisa reached over and closed the library door.

35

B RANDON WAS QUICKLY shoving papers into boxes when Prosecutor Bingley showed up unexpectedly. Sandra was not there and her cleared desktop suggested she wouldn't be returning.

From the reception, Bingley could hear a shuffling sound coming from Brandon's office. He stood in the doorway until Brandon looked up and noticed him.

"Surely, you're not moving, are you?" Bingley asked, gesturing to all the boxes stacked around Brandon's desk.

"What? Of course not," Brandon replied. "I have so many clients, it's time for a bigger office," he said.

"So, you are moving, only to a larger office," Bingley remarked with a smile and that all-too-understanding look that made Brandon uneasy, as if Bingley might know more than he was letting on.

"Well, yes," Brandon replied.

"I noticed your secretary, Sandra, is gone. She quit or just off today?"

"Can I help you?" Brandon asked like he'd just fallen from the clouds and hadn't heard the latest; the news that would surely derail his posh life.

"I've been waiting for your call. Come to see

Miss Holiday's first manuscript drafts. You've pulled them out of storage? Is that what those boxes are?"

"There's been some confusion," Brandon said.

"That happens," Bingley said and took a seat. "Tell me about it. Start from the top. I want to hear all about this

Miss Holiday."

"Miss Holiday, well, apparently she didn't write the novel. Of course, I don't know who did," Brandon plopped down in the chair across from Bingley thinking that there was no reason for him to be of concern; after all, it was Maggie who'd lied to everyone, including him. Didn't she? But is that really, truly how it all happened?

"Oh, that is confusing. Goodness, it sure is," Bingley replied.

"You see, it appears that there aren't any rough drafts of the manuscript," Brandon admitted, and that was perhaps the only honest statement he'd ever uttered, but no one was counting at this point.

"No? But you thought you had these missing drafts, didn't you? Had put them in storage, right? Let me ask you, what do you know about Miss Holiday?"

"Well, you see, that's the thing. I don't think I know much at all."

"I understand. At least I think I do," Bingley stated. "You were planning to marry her, and you're a top London agent, but still, she somehow took you to the cleaners. She deceived you, didn't she?"

"It looks as though she did. Love can be blinding," Brandon added.

"Miss Holiday was arrested, you know. Well, I guess you don't. You didn't bail her out. Of course, true love has its limits, hey? The Crown will demand that she be punished severely to set an example to all those who would steal novels and their royalties and defraud publishers."

"Well, doesn't she deserve it?" Brandon asked.

"Deserve it? And you, Sir, what do you deserve?" Bingley asked. His gaze was penetrating. Brandon shifted in his seat, yet still those eyes followed his even as he swayed side to side to deflect his gaze.

"What do you mean?" Brandon asked. "I didn't plagiarize one of the biggest selling novels ever!"

"Come now. You've admitted you're a top agent. You did no due diligence when she, an author no one had ever heard of, handed you her manuscript. All you saw was the enormous potential the novel had! Should I say, all you truly wanted to see were those vast royalties?"

"So I made a mistake!" Brandon screeched.

"No, you didn't," Bingley contradicted. "You were right all along, Sir. You are an excellent judge of what will sell. The only problem, *your* problem, I should say, is that your client did not write the novel making all the money. And that has apparently made the publishers very, very angry. They're a vengeful lot, you know."

"She lied, didn't she? Misjudging character is not against the law, if that's where you're going with this."

"Well, you see, that's exactly where the Crown is going. Sir, you defrauded a major publishing house. They don't like the smell of that. Bad for their image, you know. And you did it using Miss Holiday as your front. You used her. That's a very serious crime! Just give the publishers a ring and ask them if you deserve the same as Miss Holiday. What do you think they will say? I have a feeling they're going to want to see some blood and it just might have your name printed all over it and on both sides. You think?"

"And I did what? What? Are you charging me with something?"

"I've been a prosecutor for nearly twenty years. I know how these things are likely to go. Of course, it depends on how much the publisher wants to see you hanged. But I expect Miss Holiday's solicitor will argue, and do so convincingly, that she's a simple-minded girl—one who can't even read or write. And, you, Sir, are a slick agent. She will get a year in prison and you; I would expect ten years' hard time in His Majesty's rock yards and you can easily figure out what they spend the day doing there, can't you? Yes, indeed. I can imagine your love blindness will clear up right away when they slam a pickax in your hand."

Brandon was outraged. How did Maggie taken him in so easily? Or was it a case where greed is more blinding than love?

Prosecutor Bingley stood up glaring at Brandon.

"You used a simple-minded girl to your advantage. Juries don't like to see that, you know? I'm afraid you're likely to really annoy the court as well. But that's why the Crown keeps prisons!"

"My advantage? Do you know what grief that woman has caused me?"

"What the Crown knows is that the publisher of Miss Holidays' book paid your agency an advance of nearly a thousand pounds. Did you turn that money over to your client?"

"I was going to invest it for her. We were going to get married. I still love her," Brandon all but screeched in desperation.

"Well, of course you do, despite all the grief you now claim she has caused you. And after you're both out of prison, you're going to look her up and head straight to the church, am I right? Oh, and I did some checking into your affairs. It appears the bank was about to take away your townhouse in Kensington. You were months behind on mortgage payments, but they were all caught up about the time you signed a contract with the publisher. Did Miss Holiday's book contract help out? Is that what you were planning to invest her advance in? Your mortgage?"

"I didn't sign the contract with the publisher, Maggie did!"

"Right, that's my point. Yet Miss Holiday didn't see any of the advance, did she? I mean, not much more than lunch money doled out here and there. Which only suggests that Miss Holiday was not your accomplice, she was, indeed, your victim. Wouldn't you say? And she never knew what you had her sign as she can't read and can barely write her name."

"She tricked me!" Brandon screeched.

Bingley replied with a smirk and walked out.

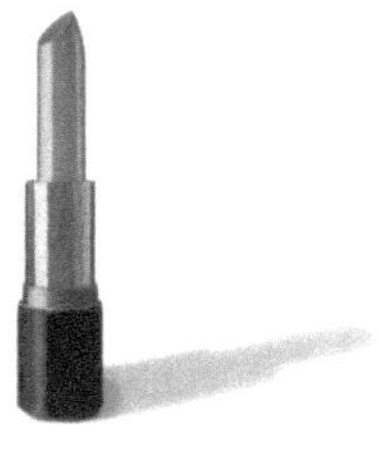

36

MARY WAS SO upset about Maggie being in jail that she could barely eat or sleep. Dora and Primrose kept vigilance by dropping by and fixing her something to eat. Sometimes they pulled the cards out to get Mary's mind off things.

Primrose was scrambling eggs for Mary when Ann brought Maggie home.

"My Mags is home!" Mary ran to embrace her daughter.

"No, Mum. It's not what you think," Maggie replied.

"Someone paid the bail so Maggie could get out. But just until the trial," Ann informed Mary.

"Mum, it was Mrs. Harold. She paid the bail," Maggie said.

"Bless you, child for bringing her home!" Mary embraced Ann.

"You see, someone convinced the prosecutors to drop the charge of fraud brought by the publishers" Ann said, "so now Maggie only has to answer to the charge of plagiarizing Peter's novel."

"I think it was someone Mrs. Harold knows," Maggie said in whispers.

"What? I don't understand," Mary said. "Aren't you home for good?"

"No, Mum."

"What is this 'plagiarism'?" Mary asked. "What does that mean? Is that some kind of crime?"

"Yes. It means I will be going to jail, Mum."

"Oh, no. It can't be!" Mary wailed.

Dora and Primrose jumped to brace Mary from collapsing to the floor.

"Mum, I didn't write the novel. You know I can't read or write," Maggie said, "That's what it means. It's Petey's novel. I stole it."

"No, you don't steal. How could you steal from Peter?" Mary asked.

"I deserve to be punished. It doesn't matter how much I regret what I did, Petey will never forgive me."

Mary broke down again.

"Go! Go and tell Peter you didn't mean it!" Mary demanded.

"Mum, Petey is prosecuting me. He signed the papers last week. Anyway, how can I say I didn't mean it when I lied to him? I took his novel that he spent years working on. I did it because I'm evil!"

"No, Mags, you're no such thing!" Mary said. "They know you didn't intend to do nothin' mean! Even if you take to acting like you're wicked girl, you've never done anything wrong in your life but shop too much!"

"Mum, I'll only be out until the trial next week," Maggie said, wiping away the tears. "I will lose the trial and they will take me back to jail from the court."

"I won't let them!" Mary yelled.

"No, Mum. I don't want you at the trial. I don't want you to see me taken away."

"Of course I'll be there. I'm your mum!"

"They'll put me in manacles. I don't want you to see that. But before I go to trial, I'm going to tell Petey how sorry I am, even though I know he hates me. Just to please you, Mum, I'll go to Petey."

* * *

Well, things happen, but not always for the best. *Perhaps*, Peter thought, *never for the best. So, is that the way life is rigged*, he wondered? Peter had made up his mind about Maggie and was long over wondering what had happened between them. There was a time he felt their dreams were intertwined, or at least they were in Peter's heart. How could she then go off and hurt him so badly simply to live the glamorous life of a celebrity?

Therefore, he was surprised when Maggie was standing outside the library at closing. She'd been there a while, perhaps working out what she'd say to him. It was raining, but Maggie had no umbrella and wore no lipstick.

Peter glanced at her but couldn't face her; not after what she'd done. He turned and headed the other way.

"Peter…" she yelled after him.

He turned but couldn't look her in the eyes. Still, he wanted to know. After all these weeks, he still couldn't sleep, wondering why she'd done what she had, and now there she stood.

"Now it's Peter… and not Petey?"

"The trial is next week," Maggie said. "You know, don't you? It doesn't matter. I don't blame you for hating me."

"You did a bad thing."

"I know Peter," Maggie said. They're going to put me in jail for a year, maybe two. That's what they told me to expect. I'm so scared. What will happen to Mum?"

Maggie fell into his arms, crying. He sheltered her with his tattered umbrella, not knowing what to do.

"What you did was wrong," he whispered, wiping the rain off her forehead and dabbing at her tears. Her soulful eyes pleaded for forgiveness. It was at that tearful moment that it all seemed to come to Peter. Yes, he realized why Maggie had done what she'd done and all the while risked turning her life upside down. He stared into her eyes until he could piece the words together to say it.

"I know you did it for Mary," Peter said and wiped his nose. "Did I tell you my mum's name was Mary? Yeah, it's true."

Peter pushed Maggie's wet hair off her forehead. Suddenly, he now saw how much more beautiful Maggie was without all the makeup, which he reasoned made her look hard at times. But she wasn't; on the contrary, she was only truly vulnerable. She'd been living day to day, wondering how Mary and her would survive and where they'd end up if life came undone for them. All the makeup was a shield to make her appear as if she were on top of the world. That place where Maggie realized she was never going to be given a second glance, even if she'd made herself a stole-away to get there.

Maggie nodded and smiled through her tears. She couldn't speak at the moment, but, yes, she'd remembered Peter's mum perished with his father in the blitz.

Still, Peter's thoughts were twisted and bruised. The pain of the moment became too great. He kissed Maggie's forehead, swallowed hard, and walked off.

Maggie called after him.

"Peter, Peter… I love you."

It was probably the most honest thing Maggie had said to him during those broken moments when they stood together in the rain..

Peter yelled back.

"I know you do!"

"Can I call you when I'm out of jail?" she pleaded through tears.

But Peter could say nothing more and kept walking. It was over for him.

37

MAGGIE WAS ORDERED to appear for trial the following week. She'd been told it would be short, which to Maggie only meant she'd be back in her cell faster. *What difference does it make?* she pondered. It was all over, and her life would be scarred forever because of her blind recklessness.

Maggie was a wreck, so anxious was she as to what would happen to Mary while she was incarcerated. Mary couldn't make rent on the flat without Maggie, and there was no one else to reach out to. It had always been Mary and Maggie—just the two of them. She was beside herself, thinking of all the things that might befall her mum.

They had assigned a special public solicitor for her, but Maggie didn't really know what was going on, only that she was headed for jail, so the details mattered little. It was a rainy dark day in more ways than one when Maggie showed up at court. The judge took the bench and called the matter.

"Gentlemen, and the Defendant," the judge began. "This case is set for trial and sentencing today. However, it appears that the case against the Defendant, who goes by the name Olivia Holiday, has unraveled. I am advised that Mr. Tinsley has unexpectedly withdrawn his charges and now indicates that he will decline to be a witness against the Defendant and will not appear. That being, there is no case and there will, therefore, be no trial. This case is dismissed."

* * *

Well, Brandon was slick. That's what made him a successful agent, he kept telling himself. Didn't he cause to be published a best-selling novel that the author hadn't written, and made a pile of money? He wasn't too worried. It was nothing more than a wee sleight-of-hand gone wrong. A fine, or two and the matter would soon enough drift away. After all, Maggie had lied to him; therefore, it was all her fault. He figured nothing would happen to him. Prosecutor Bingley was bluffing when he suggested there was likely to be a reckoning, but he wasn't. It was about come down on Brandon from all sides.

That night, Brandon had his new girlfriend over for dinner. They downed martinis as he prepared supper.

"Such a posh place. I think it's nearly as big as my father's in Belgravia." Jennifer said. "And you never see your parents?"

"Nope. Their lives are in Paris, that's where my mum is from, so it's like the place is all mine."

Jennifer looked about the gourmet kitchen, wondering what kind of parties Brandon must have for his rich and successful author clients. He'd told her all about them. Well, at least he told her the tales meant to impress her.

But then the doorbell rang.

"Get that for me, love. I ordered some wine to be delivered. I'll keep an eye on the steaks."

Brandon headed to the stove as Jennifer went for the door. She opened it for a delivery man, but there was no wine. He had a large bouquet of flowers to deliver. How nice!

"For Brandon, from his mum," the man said.

From the foyer, Jennifer yelled back to the kitchen.

"Brandon, flowers from your mum."

His mum? Brandon froze. He dropped his utensils on the floor, left the steaks to char, and dashed to the foyer screeching to Jennifer.

"Slam the door!" Brandon yelled.

But it was too late. The "delivery" man tossed the lawsuit onto the marble floor at Jennifer's feet.

"I finally got you!" he said.

"What does he mean?" Jennifer asked.

"Lawsuit is what it means! From the publisher this guy swindled."

"Who told you where I live?" Brandon demanded.

"It's on the enclosure," the man said and pulled it off the flowers and handed it to Jennifer who read it.

"I saved you a piece of my wedding cake! Love Maggie."

"Wedding cake? What wedding?" Brandon snarled. "Damn it!"

"They put a preliminary lien on this place, too. I get to file it tomorrow."

"But it's his parents' house," Jennifer said.

"Like hell it is. He owns it, and he's about to loose it! Won't need it when he's in jail!"

Brandon slammed the door in the process server's face.

"Jail?" Jennifer asked. "Who is this Maggie? Did you miss her wedding? Is that what this is all about?"

"She's the witch who put the curse on me!" Brandon replied. "I told her I wasn't going to marry her, and you can see what she's trying to do to me!"

"Really? Well, things happen, don't they?" she said. "You know, I don't think I'm hungry this evening after all," Jennifer declared before taking off her apron and tossing it at him. "Goodnight, Brandon. Don't bother to ring up!"

Jennifer stepped over the pile of flowers and headed for cover.

"What? But I love you, Jenny! And not because your daddy's rich!"

Well, maybe, but Jennifer had doubts and walked out of Brandon's life as his steaks charred and filled the kitchen with black smoke.

* * *

It wasn't long after Brandon went to jail when Peter's novel took off. The one with his name on it and not Olivia Holiday's. Sales were incredible and the strange but romantic story of Olivia Holiday, the woman who could not read or write but fell in love with her favorite author only seemed to increase sales.

Peter had earned so much money from book sales that he decided to buy himself a convertible. Well, a used one that is. Because the car was a drab gray, like his shirt, and no one wanted it so he got a particularly good price.

Peter loved to take his not so flashy convertible on long meandering drives through the countryside.

"Now that we're rich, can't we buy a new car?" Maggie asked and handed Peter a thermos tin of hot tea.

Peter pondered the question for a long time, and then pulled over to put the top down as the drizzle had stopped.

"It seems to me that we'll stay rich if we don't buy a new car," Peter said. "What do you think, Mum?"

Mary was busy in the back seat, knitting her latest sweater.

"Don't let Mags near the money!" Mary said. "She gets herself in trouble every time!"

"Hear that, love?" Peter said. "I think Mum is probably right!"

Mary held up the tiny baby's sweater she was knitting.

"Mum, I'm never going to wear that sweater!" Maggie announced, not entirely unexpectedly.

"Don't worry, Mum," Peter said. "If it's too small for the baby, I'll wear it!"

Peter patted Maggie's swollen belly. When she reached over to kiss him, his toes curled up.

THE END

For more on Justin Swingle's writings, join us at

Lewaro Road com